foster familiar
feline familiar cat cafe
book one

Rosie Pease

© 2023, Rosie Pease

All rights reserved. Except as permitted under the U.S. Copyright Act of 1976, no part of this publication may be reproduced, distributed or transmitted in any form or by any means, or stored in a database or retrieval system without the prior written permission of the publisher.

Editor: Paisley Press Books
Proofreader: Trish Long, Blossoming Pages Author Services
Cover Designer: Maria Rosera

This is a work of fiction. Names, characters, organizations, places, events, and incidents are either products of the author's imagination or are used fictitiously. Any resemblance to actual persons, living or dead, or actual events is purely coincidental.

No part of this work may be reproduced, or stored in a retrieval system, or transmitted in any form or by any means, electronic, mechanical, photocopying, recording, or otherwise, without written permission of the publisher.

PAISLEY PRESS BOOKS
WEST WARWICK, RHODE ISLAND

To all those who have ever rescued a cat.

chapter **one**

"Nora, are you sure you can handle this?" Gemma asked as she passed me the carrier. "You've never had a whole litter before."

I eyed my friend and fellow coworker and coven member as she leaned against the side of the van used by the animal rescue. "Not one this size, but I have had kittens. And it's summer. I don't have classes to worry about, so it's just work at the café and then back home to these guys. That's more time than I typically have. Besides, how hard can seven of them be?"

"Just wait until they start talking."

I held the carrier up to my face to peer in at the seven tiny furballs. Two were sleeping. Three were jockeying for prime position at the front of the cage, sticking their paws out at me, asking for attention. Two others were picking at the sides of the carrier. Even though they were small, still just eight weeks old, it had to be cramped in there. "Familiars or not, all cats talk in their own way." Familiars just happened to talk to their humans using words as well.

Gemma let out a small snort. "You've got me there. Do you have everything you need?"

I lowered the carrier as I scanned my mental list, the words

appearing in my head as if they were written on a piece of paper in front of me. Kitten food, check. Supplement if needed, check. Though given their age and healthy-looking size, I doubted they'd need it. Pet beds, cleaned and ready. Litter box, new and already prepped with litter, plus another at the ready for once they got bigger. Toys, more than I ever thought I'd need, although I'd probably end up getting more in a couple weeks once the kittens showed preferences for their favorites.

"Think so. Anything else I can grab from the store or order online." The kittens would love the boxes. Magical or not, nothing delighted a cat more than a brand-new cardboard box.

"Great! Well, after their checkup, you can take them home and let them get acclimated to your apartment."

I toed the ground. "Are you coming in with me?"

"You mean to tell me you can handle a litter of potential witch's familiars but not the vet visit?" Gemma laughed, and a few of the kittens mewed in response to the sound. "You're going to have to get over that to be a vet."

I sighed hard and scrunched my face. "They're seeing Dr. Loomis today."

Gemma brightened. "She's a great vet."

"Yeah, one who doesn't like me."

"She doesn't not like you."

I scoffed. "She could have fooled me."

Gemma placed a hand on her hip. "It doesn't help having an attitude like that."

"I do not have an attitude. She does. She's practically frigid around me."

Gemma raised an eyebrow. "You could try cutting her some slack. She's threatened by you."

I tried to restrain an eye roll. "Me? I'm no one special."

"Nora, she's the only non-magical person on staff, and

you're going to school to be a vet. You already take care of the cats at the café when they have minor issues and handle their pre-adoption wellness checks. Once you've graduated, there's no reason the coven won't get rid of her to hire you here instead."

I tugged at the collar of my hoodie, feeling slightly called out by one of my closest friends. I'd never really thought of it like that, though I questioned how true it was. Gemma was right. Dr. Loomis was a great vet. Top of her class, which I only knew because she'd gone to the same veterinary school I was now attending with two years left to go. Dr. Loomis's top marks in the licensing examination was one reason why the coven overlooked her being non-magical. Not that she knew that, I didn't think. We didn't advertise our supernatural status, though I was sure there were rumors about us all.

Although the cat café the coven ran had several non-magical baristas on staff, those who dealt with the animals directly tended to be of the witchy type just in case any of the familiars forgot they shouldn't be talking until their witch or wizard brought them home. Not that all of the cats there were familiars in waiting. They weren't. Some were truly cats. Working with the rescue to house all the cats at Feline Familiar Cat Café made our job easier. And it kept the cats—familiar or not—out of cages and in a location where they could regularly interact with our customers while they came for coffee and played any of the board games in our extensive collection.

It was a win for everyone involved. Especially for the animals needing homes.

A slight tug on my pants reminded me of the kittens in the carrier I was still holding. Still too little to talk and show that they were potential familiars, it was possible that these seven tiny creatures were all normal cats.

Then again, what cat was ever truly normal?

"I need to get these guys inside. So, are you coming with me?"

At that moment, Gemma's cell phone chimed, sending the kittens into a mewing frenzy once more. She held up a finger, telling me to wait while she checked her text.

"Sorry. Gotta go help with a rescue." She took a step forward and placed her hands on my shoulders. "You've got this. You can handle mean ol' Dr. Loomis on your own."

I cracked a smile. "So you admit that she's mean to me."

She raised her eyebrow at me once more in her signature look.

"Kidding, kidding." Kind of. "I'll try to see it from her perspective, but I make no guarantees. Good luck with the rescue."

Gemma opened the van's driver side door and got inside as I headed toward the vet's office.

chapter
two

Although the veterinary office was run by members of the local coven, it was, for all intents and purposes, a normal veterinary practice.

I opened the inner door to the building and walked to the reception desk to check in.

Tabby—a perfect name for someone who worked at the vet's—squealed as I gently set the carrier on the counter. "Oh my goodness! Look at them all. They're so cute!"

They mewed in response to Tabby's baby cooing as she wiggled her fingers in front of them, careful to not let their razor-sharp baby claws get her as the kittens reached out for her.

"Seven?" she confirmed as she plopped back into her chair behind the computer, looking at me expectantly.

I nodded.

"Any names?"

"Not yet. Gotta get to know them first. Gemma just handed them over to me in the parking lot." When it came to familiars, sometimes they kept the names you gave them, and other times, they told you their names instead.

Outside of seeing their photo when I initially said yes to fostering the litter, this was my first good look at them all.

Five tiny sets of eyes peered out at me. A different two than before were curled up in the corner and couldn't be bothered by what was going on around them. Two black, one black and white cow cat, a calico, and three tabbies, two orange and a brown.

"Age?"

"Eight weeks-ish, maybe nine."

"Dr. Loomis might have a better idea."

So would I once I saw them out of the carrier. They were still too little for me to ask outright. Not that I'd do that out here in the lobby where humans, witches, and their pets sat waiting to be seen.

"How is she today?" Working the front desk, Tabby knew everything about everyone. Or at least tried to. That included my feelings about Dr. Loomis and hers about me.

"Better." Then she stood and leaned over the desk to whisper, "I think she and her husband finally made up."

Not that I knew she was married until now, but, "Were they having problems?"

Her eyes went wide as she shrugged in an exaggerated fashion. "She was spending a lot of late nights here. Staff had to keep telling her to go home."

"Oh." That was more information than I knew what to do with. "Well, better bodes well for me, I guess."

Tabby smiled and plopped back into her seat. She clicked one final thing on her computer, then looked back up at me. "Okay, you can take a seat, and one of the techs will grab you shortly."

Thanking her, I turned toward the feline waiting area. For the most part, they separated the dogs from the cats and other small animals. The practice saw nearly every type of animal that could be a pet, though the less common ones were pretty much guaranteed to be familiars. Their ability to talk about their own health needs made taking care of them a lot easier. There were other vets we could refer nonfamiliars to when needed.

I sat down and placed the carrier on the floor between my legs. Next to me, a woman sat on her phone with her cat carrier sitting on the seat beside her. I tried peeking in but had no luck seeing whoever was inside. Beyond her were a few more people and their cats, and one rabbit. Likely a familiar. To test, I nodded at the fluffy white and orange bunny. It nodded back. Thought so. I did the same to the witch when she caught me looking, and she returned a smile. She looked familiar. Maybe a hedge witch who rarely came to coven gatherings or a customer from the café. I had what most people called a photographic memory, but I had to concentrate to recall the everyday sort of stuff that I tried not to pay too much attention to.

Sometime after the witch and her bunny were called into one room, I was called into the other. I grabbed the kitten-filled carrier and hurried across the waiting area to the open door being held open for me by the tech.

Morgan grinned widely as I passed by, eyeing the carrier with excitement. A year ahead of me, she was one of my favorite techs here, probably anywhere. We'd even lived together for a short time in grad student housing on campus, which is where I'd found out she was a witch and brought her into our coven. If she hadn't moved in with her boyfriend, we might still have been living together now.

We exchanged pleasantries, and as soon as the door closed, she asked, "What do you think their chances are?"

"Just met them outside, but let's get a good look and

maybe you can tell me." I set the carrier on the exam room table and then unlatched the front.

Three kittens spilled out as I opened the door. The two orange tabbies and the cow cat. A black kitten hesitantly came out next but soon joined the others in exploring the carrier. The calico initially seemed like she was coming, poking her head out to investigate, but she took a few sniffs of the air, then turned back around as if she was too good for this scene. Moments later, the other two kittens sleepily emerged. I peeked in to see the calico getting comfortable in what had been their spot.

"We can let the other one be for now," Morgan said. "We have our hands full enough already."

Morgan pulled a paper from her upper coat pocket and unfolded it. I immediately recognized the coven's logo. A half snowflake representing our home of Snowhaven acting as the top of a tree of life. "Have you done one of these yet?" she asked me as she began to scrawl a few notes on top. She giggled as the once-sleepy brown tabby took interest in the pen's movement, extending its head to sniff the moving top and then batting the tip as Morgan wrote.

I shook my head as I corralled an orange kitten from jumping off the exam table while the other sniffed at my shirt collar, standing on its hind legs to do so while using its front to brace itself on my chest. "Not an initial one. Any I've done have been for known familiars."

She slid the paper to me. "Not much different in the beginning than a standard vet form that I complete in there." She pointed to the laptop on the rolling cart next to her, then moved the wireless mouse to wake the screen up. "The usual vitals, temperament description, that sort of thing. There will be one for each kitten, but I'll transfer all that over tonight and forward you copies. I assume they sent you observation forms."

I perused the form as I pet the cow cat who had come over to help its sibling investigate my shirt. Although the orange tabby continued to do so, the cow cat now just sat and stared at me. "Yeah. Those I've had for other fosters." This may have been my first big litter, but I'd been taking one or two at a time since moving into my apartment as something to do and to give my own kitty familiar the occasional company.

"Great, then this should be a piece of cake." She scooped up the brown tabby. "And you can go first since you won't leave me alone." She lifted his tail to confirm he was a boy and then plopped him onto the scale on the counter. He mewed in protest. "Oh, I know, so cold," she cooed as she comforted the little tabby, then reached back for her clipboard so she could record his weight. Battling my keys and wallet, I retrieved my pen from the front pouch of my hoodie—a barista was never far away from something to write with—and recorded the kitten's weight on the coven form.

Together we made quick work of processing the kittens, and all too soon, Morgan was gone, leaving me and the litter to wait for Dr. Loomis.

chapter
three

Keeping kittens contained on the exam table proved to be a futile effort. The moment I'd scoot to grab one from going off the edge, another would try to jump from the table to the corner counter where supplies lined the back wall. So I sat on the small two-person bench set against the wall and waited for the vet to come in while the kittens explored both the room and me.

As if on cue, Dr. Loomis walked in with the laptop cart as I was cleaning a piddle puddle on the floor. Of course.

She barely gave me a passing glance. "You let them run free while you waited?"

"Glad I did, or else we'd be giving them all a bath right now." I stood and dropped the dirty paper towels into the hole in the counter above the trash can. A minute prior and she would have seen a completely different scene—two kittens on my lap, another next to me—instead of the chaos now that had resumed only because I'd moved. "Not that it would have made much sense for me to stress them out by putting them in the carrier only to take them back out again." Besides, letting them roam helped familiarize them with the space and hopefully led to less frightening visits in the future.

Without another word, she surveyed the exam room as I washed my hands. Outside of finding the jar of long cotton swabs slightly shifted from the rest of the containers thanks to one of the black kittens slinking behind it moments before, nothing was out of place. Minus the bottle of disinfectant because of the piddle, of course. I bent to grab it, then put it back in the bottom cupboard.

The black kitten sat next to me beside the sink, staring at Dr. Loomis. She seemed to soften at the sight of him. She wiggled a finger in front of him, and he approached to smell it.

"Aren't you a sweetie?" On the floor, the brown tabby, the piddler, rubbed against her shoe. "You too. Which one of you wants to go first?"

The black kitten jumped down from the counter as if knowing what she'd said. Maybe he did. We still weren't sure just when familiars became aware of what we were saying, though we knew they didn't start to talk until around sixteen weeks.

She scooped the piddler up off the floor as the cow cat scooted out of reach. "That answers that," she said softly, almost with a little chuckle at the end. As she walked around me, the kitten melted into her hands, even as Dr. Loomis shifted first to dangle her over the exam table, letting her feet sway, then cradling her like a baby. "Great temperament. Where did they come from?"

I took a few steps back to the bench and sat down. "Cat colony at the amusement park. They all just showed up last week."

Dr. Loomis glanced at me curiously. "Any sign of Mom?"

I shook my head. "Complete surprise to the staff there. The

rescue has worked with them extensively the last couple of years to TNR the entire colony." The trap, neuter (or spay), and release of the semi-feral cats allowed them to remain where they were comfortable without increasing the population.

She *mmm*ed. "I've fixed several of them myself. Perhaps they were dumped there." She gently pulled the kitten's skin between her shoulders near the scruff, then let go, checking for signs of dehydration. It snapped back into place. Completely normal. "Good of whoever to at least wait until they'd had their needed time with Mom."

This was the most we'd spoken to one another in one go in a long time. Maybe Gemma was right and I just needed to cut her some slack. "So we're right at eightish weeks?"

"For sure. No more than ten." She smiled at me. Actually smiled. I couldn't remember the last time that happened. Scratch that. I could. It was the last vet visit I'd made with one of the café cats before Dr. Loomis came to speak to my class and saw me sitting there among the students. I waved. She barely acknowledged me. And after that, she was different at future vet visits.

Dr. Loomis reached into a drawer and pulled out a thermometer. After prepping it, she took the brown tabby's temperature with little protest. "Great temperament. And you are all set for the time being." With one hand, she set the thermometer aside on the counter and released the kitten with the other. She typed something into the computer, then eyed the remaining kittens with warm tenderness. She really was good with them. "Okay, who's next?"

It was two kittens later that Dr. Loomis smiled at me again. And this time, I saw it. The green between her teeth. It wasn't an uncommon sight at the cat café and was something that happened to everyone on occasion, but I hated being the one to spot it. I always felt weird calling attention to it, but did because I could only hope someone would do the same for me.

"Got a little something right there." I pointed to my upper teeth.

"Ugh . . ." Dr. Loomis turned and smiled wide into the metal box on the wall that held the stack of brown paper towels. She tried using her tongue to dislodge the offending greenery, but to no avail. "Thanks. I had this amazing salad for lunch today."

While examining the first black kitten, she went on to tell me all about this strawberry summer salad with a balsamic and maple vinaigrette dressing. It sounded delicious. I'd have to tell Amy at the café about the combo. She loved to add new things to the menu to switch things up and keep customers coming. As if the cats and board games didn't do it already, Amy's food would. Wouldn't be surprised if she was a kitchen witch, though she'd never come out and said so.

"Of course," Dr. Loomis continued, "the problem with salad for lunch is falling victim to stuff like this. That's what I get for trying to eat healthy."

"Maybe you should toss the salad next time instead." I cracked a smile.

She just blinked at me.

"Get it? Toss? Tossed salad?"

But nothing. After a quick cuddle post temperature check, she set the black kitten aside and then typed something into the computer. She glanced at me curiously.

Guess we weren't at the cracking jokes stage of our tenuous relationship yet. I pulled on the collar of my hoodie, now uncomfortable as I sat there.

"Little warm for a sweatshirt, isn't it?" she asked cooly.

And there was the attitude I'd grown so accustomed to, the

air of judgment around what she said as she spoke to me. I almost regretted that I'd told her about the piece of lettuce. Truthfully, yes, it was too hot for a sweatshirt, but I wasn't going to agree with her outright. Besides, "It's good protection from their claws." Which was the whole reason I'd chosen to wear it this morning. "And then where else would this little guy have gotten to sleep?" I lifted the orange kitten, who had been so interested in my collar earlier, out of my hood.

She reached out for him. "Guess this makes him my next patient."

I handed him to her, and as she lifted the kitten out of my grasp, the weight of the awkwardness between us settled in.

chapter
four

The next several weeks went by a little faster than they usually did. Between veterinary classes and my shifts at Feline Familiar, I'd been busy looking after the kittens and socializing them, with a few visits from Gemma to help with that. In another week or so, they'd start to talk if they were destined to become familiars. It was the main reason why we didn't integrate kittens into the café's catio as soon as other groups might have. The extra chattiness of the newly vocal drew extra attention to the kitten familiars, even more than if they were normal kittens. We couldn't have them figuring out how to talk in front of our non-magical customers. Not that they all would have heard the kittens actually speaking, but it was always a possibility, more so if someone didn't know they had magical ancestry—and that was a whole different worry that we didn't want to deal with. So fostering longer made the transition to talking as comfortable a process for everyone, allowing the new familiars to settle into their abilities and learn the rules that would keep them safe.

Although at least some of my seven were expected to become familiars, they were first and foremost cats physically.

They were getting to a certain age, which meant it was time for them to get fixed, starting with the three boys: Batley, Dodger, and Sport. Once they recuperated, they'd go to the café so that when the girls had their turn, the apartment would be quieter for their recovery.

"Gotta get up. The kittens have a big day," Alphie, my curmudgeonly familiar, said as he tapped my nose while I tried to wake up. It was never a pretty sight. There was a reason I had become a barista. I needed my coffee. And preferably lots of it. And between working at the café and serving as the on-site veterinary assistant for the café cats, I got a pretty good staff discount.

I dug my fingers into my long-haired tuxedo as he sat on my chest. "You sound almost disappointed that they're going to be gone for the day. You know they're coming back for at least a few days after this, right? They need to recuperate, and we still need to wait until they talk."

"I wouldn't say disappointed. I'm happy to get my spot back."

"Your spot?" I sputtered a laugh as I rolled over. "You never lost your spot."

"I've had to share it."

"Don't say you haven't enjoyed that. I've seen you giving all of them baths there." That had been my one fear about fostering a whole litter, that it would be too much for Alphie. I'd told him several times that all he had to do was say the word and I'd go back to fostering quieter singles and pairs—familiars or not—those needing to come out of their shells versus rambunctious kittens causing all sorts of mischief. But he'd taken it all in stride.

"Not that spot. My other one." Oh, the one at the top of the old recliner. "It was fine when they couldn't get up, but now it's like they're mountain climbers racing to the top. I'm old. I like my sleep."

"The boys might be sleepier than usual the next couple of days."

"That will be nice. Now come on"—he tapped my nose again—"I made you some coffee."

He hadn't actually. I had the coffee maker set on a timer, but he took pride in watching the coffee drip into the pot every morning. He called it magic how I put water into it at night and it came out as coffee. No matter how many times he turned the faucet on to drip, he couldn't get it to be anything but water.

I opened the bedroom door to a crowd of kittens waiting for me and Alphie. That had been my one rule about fostering. No kittens on the bed. It wasn't so much that I didn't want them there—I loved cuddling with Alphie—but I didn't want the kittens to learn that the bed was okay only for whoever they went home with to not want them on their bed. They had the run of everywhere else, but only Alphie could go into my room thanks to the cat door and a special charm on his collar that allowed the door to open for him. More magic, he called it. It amused me how he would call modern technology magic when he was a witch's familiar. Then again, most of my magic was all in my head, so it wasn't like he was helping me with spells and the like. The most he got to do for me in that respect was turn on the faucet so I could prep my moon water each month.

"Good morning, everyone." I squatted to pet the lot as Alphie used the distraction to get around them all without stopping. "How are you all? Hungry, I bet." They hadn't been able to have anything after midnight last night. I'd get the girls some food once the boys were in the carrier just before leaving.

I put Dodger, one of the black kittens, on one shoulder

and Whisk, the female orange tabby, on the other. Whisk would have preferred being in my hood, had I had one on, but the shoulder was the next best spot. Then I picked up Tilly, the cow cat, and cradled her like a baby with one arm as I stood. The others followed me into the kitchen and toward the coffee.

Tilly rolled out of my arms as I reached the counter and scampered over toward Alphie, who was in the sink drinking out of the faucet. He preferred his water that way, and Tilly had quickly followed suit upon watching him. Since she wasn't going to the vet's today, she was fine to have a drink.

I prepped my coffee as the kittens begged for some breakfast. "Soon, soon," I promised them. I felt almost guilty reaching into my cupboard for the plain croissant Amy had sent me home with yesterday. There'd been a few extras in the case once we closed down for the evening, so she'd split them among everyone on the shift. Another perk of working at the café beyond the coffee. I cut it open, then added some ham and cheese onto it before sticking it into the microwave to heat.

Once it was done, I headed over to my old recliner and sat as both Whisk and Dodger hopped to the top of the plush blue chair. The other kittens piled onto my lap or the recliner arms, and we remained that way for several minutes as I caught up on the morning headlines on TV while I ate.

"Shouldn't you be going?" Alphie called as he sauntered into the living room with Tilly right behind him. The two black and white cats made a cute pair. One furry in formal wear and the other sleek with large black spots dotting her body.

"Just getting up. Don't worry." I lifted two cuddly kittens off my lap toward the chair arms, knowing they'd roll back into the chair to soak up its warmth, then stood up.

I quickly got dressed, then pulled the cat carrier out of the closet, already prepped with a towel in there for comfort.

Foster Familiar

Although the carrier was a common sight for them all, even Alfie's head popped up as I brought it into the living room before he settled back in, eyes on it to watch the show. Try as I might to get the kittens all used to being put in the carrier on the regular so that it wasn't a scary experience for them, corralling even a few of them at one time was humorous.

Batley was, by far, the easiest. Named for his oversized ears that reminded me of bat wings, I simply picked the black kitten up and placed him inside before he could realize what I'd done.

Sport went in next, lured in by a laser light and a toy tossed into the carrier at the last moment so he wouldn't continue to search the towel or his brothers for the red dot. He'd follow it anywhere.

That left Dodger. There was a reason he had received that name, and it had nothing to do with baseball. Until I learned that he much preferred to ride on my back or shoulder, he had dodged nearly every attempt of mine to pick him up or hold him, and he'd wriggle out of my grasp those rare times I did manage to get him.

First, the sneak approach as he sniffed at his brothers in the carrier. One of them must have given me away, and he hopped over the carrier to the other side.

The jig was up. "Come on, Dodge. You're next." I stepped around the carrier.

He bounded to the top of the recliner and waited until he was within arm's reach before leaping off the back. He sped up the short hallway, and I followed him, closing the door to my bedroom as I passed so he couldn't veer in there to go hide under the bed where I'd never be able to get him. Then he ran back past me and onto the kitchen counter, where he stopped and waited for me yet again.

"Can't you do something?" I asked Alphie, who watched the show from his spot by the window.

"Like what? I've never been good at catching him either."

I reached for the medium-haired black cat once more, but he darted toward the cat tree. In one hole at the side and out of the hole on top, he leaped to the scratching post and climbed into the top basket before jumping to the bookcase, where he stared at me triumphantly as if to say he'd won this round. My fingertips could barely reach the top of the bookcase, never mind attempt to get around him. Not without the possibility of knocking things off of it or worse.

"Come on, Dodger. Please?" I said, exasperated by his evasive maneuvers. He looked at me then, and instead of leaping off the bookcase as I assumed he would, he reached out toward me. I went toward him, and he jumped onto my shoulder and balanced there.

I opened the top door to the carrier and placed him inside, using him to block his brothers from hopping back out, then latched the door closed. "Really? It was that simple? I just had to say please?"

Alphie laughed. "Guess it really is a magic word."

I nodded. No way was he not going to be a familiar after that revelation. I picked up the carrier, lighter than it had been in some time without all the kittens in there, and walked over with it to the door. Then I returned to the kitchen and grabbed the kitten food and filled two bowls for the girls before setting a bowl of cat food out for Alphie. The boys mewed in protest and let me know of their displeasure all the way down the stairs, to the car, and during the ride to the vet's.

chapter
five

Although the kitten wrangling had seemed to take far too long, I was right on time for when I was supposed to drop the boys off. The office was still closed for another hour to office visits, but I had permission to bring the boys in early for their surgery before I headed to work. This wasn't some special treatment because I was a coven member or worked with the rescue. They allowed anyone to drop their pets off early the morning of surgery.

I pulled into a spot at the front of the building and cut the engine. The moment the car went quiet, so did the kittens. Longest drive ever.

"We're here," I told them in a voice I hoped sounded reassuring and not a bit hesitant about what was to come. They'd come to the vet's several times since I first got them, about every two weeks, and they hadn't been like this before. But all those other times, it had been as part of a group of seven, not three. Maybe that was the issue. "You'll see your sisters later today."

I got out of the car and walked around to the back passenger-side seat where I'd secured the carrier. They seemed okay, no accidents from what I could see, thank goodness, so I unbuckled the carrier and headed for the office door.

Since it wasn't open, I pressed the buzzer to alert the vet—Dr. Loomis again—that I needed to be let in. After a minute without an answer, I buzzed again. When she still didn't come to the door, I held the button down. If I remembered correctly, this had two-way communication.

"Hey, it's Nora here with the boys for their neuter today. Dr. Loomis?"

When there was still no answer, I set the carrier on the ground and grabbed my phone to call inside. No one answered that either. Though given I was here before the office staff arrived, that wasn't out of the ordinary. Not knowing what else to do, I texted one of my professors who also was part of the practice here.

ME

> No one's answering the clinic door. I'm here for a surgical drop-off.

BARKER

> Strange. Dr. Loomis should be there. I'll call her cell.

Less than half a minute later, my phone buzzed with an incoming call.

"No answer," Dr. Barker said in lieu of a greeting, her voice concerned. "Head around back, will you? I don't like this."

I didn't like it either. She didn't need to tell me twice. "Absolutely." I picked up the cat carrier and started to walk around the building. Dr. Loomis had a reputation, and it didn't include not showing up to work.

Dr. Barker stayed on the line as I hurried down the side of

the building, careful not to jostle the carrier too much. One of the kittens mewed unhappily. "Shh . . . almost there."

"Are you talking to me?"

"No, the kittens. I wasn't going to leave them by the door or put them back in the warm car." Finally, I turned the corner, and I had to hold the carrier straight out in front of me to squeeze between the building and the row of hedges behind it. "This building is deceptively long."

"When you only approach it from one way all the time, you never get a real idea of how big it is. There's always a lot more going on than what you see."

"This sounds like one of your lessons."

"Maybe it was. Where are you now?"

"Walking around the outdoor dog run. Okay. Now I'm in the parking lot." And so was one lonely car pulled into a spot close to the back door. "Is Loomis's car red?"

"Yes. Some sporty thing."

"Then she should be here." And inside since she wasn't in the car or waiting by the door.

"I don't know if that makes me feel better or worse."

I pressed the phone to my shoulder with my head as I switched the carrier to the other hand. It was getting heavy. "I'm almost to the door."

"Good. Maybe she was just in the bathroom."

I hoped so, but as I got closer to the entrance, I doubted it. "The door's open."

"You mean like it's unlocked?"

"No. Open, open. As in, she didn't close it behind her."

"That's not like her at all."

"I'm going in." I bumped the door open further with my hip and called inside the lit entry hallway, "Dr. Loomis?"

"Do be careful."

"I will."

A glass wall lined one side of the hallway. The room inside was home to the lab where samples were run and also where medicines were stored. She wasn't in there, and I didn't see her through the glass in the main room, where cages stood empty and waiting for patients recuperating after procedures. The opposite hallway wall hid the operating room on the other side and blocked the rest of the room and access to the exam rooms from view. I came around the corner and turned toward the OR and exam rooms. No one was in sight, but Dr. Loomis's take-home container of salad sat on the counter leading to the OR. So she hadn't made it to the staff refrigerator.

"Dr. Loomis?"

I set the carrier on the ground and continued the few feet to the OR. The door struck an overturned metal tray on the floor as I pushed my way inside. Dr. Loomis lay face down, tools from the metal tray scattered around her.

"I found Dr. Loomis." Before Dr. Barker could say anything, I added, "She's dead."

chapter
six

"Call the police," Dr. Barker ordered. "I'm on my way. Be there soon."

She ended the call, and I brought it down from my ear. The screen quickly turned black, prompting me back into action. The thought crossed my mind to use the office's phone to call 911, but that would have required me to go further into the room, and I didn't want to do that. I clicked my phone back on and brought up the call screen and pressed 911.

"911. What's your emergency?"

"I'm at the Familiar Friends Animal Hospital on Squall Street. I found a body. The vet, one of them, Dr. Loomis is dead in the back room."

"Have you checked the victim to ensure they're dead?"

Oh my gosh, I hadn't, just froze and assumed. I was the absolute worst. I rushed to Dr. Loomis and checked her pulse. There wasn't one. I told the operator that, then after a breath added, "I'm training to be a vet. I know how to check."

"Did you work with the victim?"

Every hair rose on my body. *Victim?* Had someone done something to Dr. Loomis?

I gave her body a once over, coming to a stop by her hip farthest from me where a notebook poked out from under her body. It must have fallen out of a pocket. I peeked at it. The name Dodger was visible on the page facing up. Was this my Dodger? Why was his name in her notebook? Ones like this weren't used here. The animal hospital was practically paperless aside from the initial potential familiar intake forms used by the coven. And speaking of the coven, was that? It was. A simple sketch of the logo for the Snowhaven Coven. Not thinking, I pulled it the rest of the way out from under her. Flipping it over, the other page had Sport written on it, again with the coven symbol. This was no coincidence. My fosters were in this notebook.

Outside of the notebook, I saw nothing out of the ordinary, no injuries, at least from behind. I knew enough from crime shows that I shouldn't roll her over. That would contaminate more evidence than I needed to . . . more than I already had.

"Ma'am? Are you still there?"

"Yeah, sorry. No, I mean kind of? But not today. I was dropping off my fosters to be fixed." I continued my explanation as if the operator really cared. But she'd probably heard it all from everyone. I couldn't be the only one who rambled in these sorts of situations.

"Help is on the way," the operator assured me, "you should hear sirens any second now. Please make sure any animals are contained."

"They're in a carrier, but I'll move it from the door."

"Do you need me to stay on the line?"

"No. It's okay. I should probably call work and let them know I'm going to be late. Thank you."

Like the operator had said would happen any moment, the

sound of sirens infiltrated the space, far away at first. I momentarily froze as I looked down at the notebook in my hand. This was evidence. I was sure of it. But it was also evidence that could reveal the truth about my foster kittens. That they—at least some of them—would become familiars. It was my duty to protect them. And if that meant interfering with this investigation, then so be it.

I pocketed the notebook, then quickly backed out of the operating room and into the hallway to grab the cat carrier. The kittens sounded their own alarm, likely unhappy with both the increasing volume of the sirens and still being cramped together in the small space.

"Soon, soon," I said, my voice soft, though I wasn't sure what I was promising. The end to the noise or that they'd be out of the carrier. With Dr. Loomis dead, there was no telling when they'd have their surgery now, but it wouldn't be today.

I stepped back out of the entry hall, wanting to provide ample room for whoever would be coming through the doors any minute. Not knowing where to go, I inched along the perimeter of the room, away from Dr. Loomis, my gaze darting around the room as I tried to look anywhere but toward the OR. I didn't want the sight burned into my memory any more than it would be already.

The sirens abruptly cut out, and the kittens' cries followed, only for them to start up again the moment the door to the outside opened and a male officer announced, "Snowhaven PD. Is anyone in the building?"

"I'm to your left," I called out, now pressed up against the cages at the front of the room. "The body is to your right as you enter."

"Is anyone else with you?"

"Three unhappy kittens in a carrier."

The officer appeared at the end of the hallway just then. "Are you safe?"

I nodded, and the officer quickly surveyed the scene as who I assumed was his partner filed in behind him, ushering a pair of EMTs inside. The EMTs quickly diverted to the body, while the officer who came in first crossed over to me.

"Officer Duvall." He stuck out his hand.

I shifted the carrier to my left hand and shook his with my right. "Nora. Where should I be? I need to get these guys out of the carrier." And fed now that surgery was off the table.

"We'll have some questions for you, no doubt. Is there a room we can go to, to get you out of the way? You don't need to see this." As he spoke, the EMTs moved away from Dr. Loomis, confirming what I already knew to the other officer with a shake of their heads.

"A little late for that," I said to Officer Duvall at the same time as I heard my name called from outside. "Dr. Barker."

"Is that the deceased?"

"No. That's who yelled for me. She works here. Another vet." She really had gotten here quickly. Though I guess that shouldn't have been a surprise. She was probably already in her car on her way to work when I texted about the door being locked.

"One moment." He crossed the room once more and said a few words to his partner before disappearing down the hall. A few minutes passed, and he appeared from one of the exam rooms. "Follow me. You can bring the kittens."

"Thank you." I followed him into the exam room but quickly said "Not this one" when it seemed like he was going to leave me inside.

He quirked an eyebrow.

"It's a dog room. They keep them separate to decrease

anxiety in the animals. The cat ones are on that wall." I pointed diagonally across the room as if he could see through to where I meant.

He nodded, then ushered me out the other door into the front of the practice.

There, Dr. Barker and Tabby rushed over to me, taking the officer by surprise. Dr. Barker pulled me in for a hug, leaving me awkwardly extending the carrier away from my side. "Oh, you poor thing. Are you all right?"

"Please, step back," the officer insisted. "The witness will be able to talk to you after." Dr. Barker froze, then slowly lifted her hands up and away before stiffly taking a step backward.

I gave her a sympathetic smile and then one to Tabby as Dr. Barker searched my face. "I'm okay," I mouthed, but that wasn't entirely true. The pit that had settled in my stomach upon finding Dr. Loomis and the operator calling her a victim took root inside me. Witness. Like this wasn't some sort of horrible accident or natural medical emergency. It had to be one of the two, right, or did they know something I didn't? At this stage, how could they?

Officer Duvall cleared his throat and waited for me to take a step before turning away from us to lead the way toward the exam room door. He opened it, and upon giving it a cursory inspection, let me go inside and then followed me in.

"Please do not leave the room."

"Can I let the kittens out now? Maybe get a litter box and some food? They were supposed to have surgery—"

The officer held up his hand. "As long as you can keep them under control and prevent them from getting out of this room, I'll have someone come in with what you need."

"Thank you, thank you." The kittens seemed pleased with

this announcement too. One let out a single meow and extended his paw through the cage.

The officer's voice softened as he said, "I know how mine gets when she wants food. Starts finding all the things she shouldn't be eating to let me know."

I'd heard that a time or two from customers at the café. It made me glad that Alphie could just tell me he was getting hungry without having to resort to such measures. "They get into everything, don't they? The amount of kitten-proofing I had to do beyond what I thought for these guys and their sisters was something else."

"Plastic bags." He shook his head. "I don't get the appeal. Kinda makes you wish you could ask why they like them so much."

"Yeah. Wouldn't that be something?" My glance shot to the carrier still in my hand. If he only knew that for some cats, asking just that and more was not only possible but probable, and that three who could maybe someday answer him were in the room with us.

"Well, someone will be in to talk with you soon. Sit tight."

"Thanks again," I said as Officer Duvall left the room the way we had come in.

Once he pulled the door closed, I set the carrier on the exam room table and opened the latch. Sport pushed through, his toy in his mouth, followed by Dodger and Batley. "Please do not try to leave the room when the door opens again, go back into the carrier if I tell you to"—I looked sternly at Dodger but meant what I said next for all three of them—"and do not make me chase you around in here." The room was small, but there were plenty of things they could knock over during a getaway attempt.

"Okay, we won't," came the tiny voice out of Dodger.

chapter
seven

I stared at the black kitten. "You just talked."

"I know," he said proudly. "But you knew that could happen. That's why you have us in the first place."

"But it's too soon. I didn't expect it for another few weeks."

"Happens early sometimes."

"Is it going to happen to all of you?" My gaze darted between the other two kittens on the table.

Dodger flopped his head this way and that to glance at his brothers before returning his attention to me. "No. Not early, and not at all." Batley seemed unbothered by the turn of events, sniffing all around the exam table and the carrier. Sport, who had initially dropped his toy upon his brother speaking, had resumed batting it between his paws. He sent it tumbling off the table and went after it.

"Okay, then." Well, that complicated things, especially in this situation. "New rule. And this one is really important. No talking to the other humans here, especially any dressed like the man who brought us in here. Got it?" I did not want to be responsible for exposing the witchy world to the Snowhaven PD.

"Got it. Are we really going to eat soon? I'm starving."

"I hope so." He seemed contented by this and jumped down toward Sport and his toy.

Could the timing of him now being able to talk be any worse? With us in here and a whole investigation going on in the next room?

The thought flitted through my mind that yes, it could. Had this been a routine drop-off, Dodger might have talked to Dr. Loomis right before surgery. What a mess that would have been. What were they thinking, having a non-magical vet work on kittens this close to speaking age? Given everything that happened, guess that wasn't a concern anymore.

Poor Dr. Loomis. We might not have been close, but she was a brilliant vet, and her life had been cut far too short. What had happened to her?

My cell phone vibrated in my pocket, reminding me of one important thing I'd forgotten to do amidst all the hubbub of the morning.

It apparently was not the first time it had gone off.

> **GEMMA**
>
> I know you said you were going to be late this morning, but I thought you were talking about minutes. Everything go okay with the drop-off?
>
> Okay, now it's really late. Where are you?
>
> We just got a call about the police response at the vet's office. You call me this instant!

I doubted it would be a good idea to call. I didn't even

know if it was okay for me to have my phone. Not that anyone had said otherwise. But I had to text her at least to keep her from worrying any longer.

> ME
> Sorry!!! I'm okay.

Oh thank the Goddess! What's going on? No one is answering the office line. We can't reach anyone.

> I don't know how much I'm allowed to say.

What does that mean??

She wasn't going to let this go. Not that I would have either if the roles were reversed.

> Dr. Loomis is dead.

WHAT?!

> I found her when I came to drop off the boys.

Oh my Goddess! Tell me everything!

I was partway through my explanation when a soft knock sounded on the door coming from the back room.

Sliding the phone back into my pocket, I said, "Come on in, watch the kittens." To them, I added, "Away from the door."

Dodger batted the toy across the floor, sending Sport after it and out of the door's path as it slowly opened.

A man in plain clothes shuffled in, bent over, one hand extended down to help block the door. Impressive. He had to have animals himself. He made his way through the door, revealing an overwhelming bundle of stuff haphazardly tucked under his arm.

"Here, let me help you with that." I rushed the few steps to grab a small bag of cat food before it could fall to the floor.

"Thank you," he said, straightening and using his foot to knock the door closed. "Everyone accounted for?"

A quick scan revealed all three boys eyeing our visitor from their spots in the room with interest. Even Sport had momentarily lost interest in his toy.

"All here." Now that he was upright, I could get a good look at him. About my age, average height, blondish-brown hair that was somewhere between not too short but not shaggy, slightly smaller than average frame, but his long-sleeved, collared shirt and khaki pants hid anything more. I knew him from somewhere, most likely the café, and I searched my brain for the name I knew was there. "Thank you for this."

"You're welcome." He set a small litter pan that had been tucked under his arm on the exam table, letting everything else he'd been holding against it fall into the shallow basin. "You have the food, and here's some litter, bowls, and I brought canned food too—wasn't sure what they eat."

"Oh, just about everything I give them. And some of them eat things I don't give them too."

"Cardboard?"

"Yours too?"

He studied me for a moment. "How'd you know?"

"The way you walked in here."

He smiled sheepishly. "I have a runner."

I pointed at Dodger, who had jumped up on the table to investigate what was there. "So is that one."

The man extended an arm toward Dodger and wiggled his fingers. Dodger momentarily feigned interest in favor of the stuff inside the litter pan but soon came to sniff his fingers. And when those fingers turned to give him some chin scratches, he stayed for more.

"Not running now, are you?" The man smiled again, the corners of his eyes crinkling. "I think he likes me."

"He'll be looking for a home in a couple weeks."

"Oh, I, uh—"

"Sorry." I held up a hand at chest height as if to say my bad and wave the suggestion away. "Force of habit. I'm fostering him and his siblings. There are four girls back home."

"Oh, wow. Seven, huh? So that's what brought you to the vet today?"

"Yeah. They were supposed to get fixed this morning."

"Poor guys." He chuckled as he continued to pet Dodger, then looked back at me and stopped. "Sorry, bad joke. I know how important it is to spay and neuter your pets. Bob Barker told me so."

Now it was me who chuckled, or was that a giggle? It was a little higher in pitch than my typical laugh. "I loved watching that show as a kid on snow days."

The man looked at me, hard and long enough for his fingers to stop petting Dodger, who headbutted him. As if not thinking, the man reached for Dodger and picked him up. The kitten, who got his name from his regular evasion tactics, simply allowed it, stunning me as he further permitted himself to be held like a baby as the man resumed petting him once more.

"Do I know you?" he asked.

"I'm a barista over at Feline Familiar, the cat—"

"Café. I know it well. Forgive my manners, I'm—"

"Grant." Knew I'd remember it with enough time.

His head ticked to the side. "You know all of your customers' names?"

"If not that, then their orders. So many are creatures of habit. Not you, though. You switch it up regularly, but I can see myself writing your name on the side of your to-go cup." I tapped my head. "Photographic memory."

"Neat," he sounded genuinely impressed. "That would come in so handy for work."

"What do you do? Are you an officer?" Why else would he be here?

He shook his head. "Crime scene tech."

"Oh, wow."

"Yeah. That's the other reason they sent me in here. I've been tasked with getting your statement."

"Right." The levity that he'd brought into the room dampened as I remembered why I was here like this. "I don't think I know much to help you. What you saw is what I walked into."

Grant stopped petting Dodger and tried to put him down. Dodger wasn't having any of that and instead spun out of Grant's grasp and climbed his way onto Grant's shoulder before draping himself over it.

Grant shrugged and pulled a tape recorder and a notebook and pen from his back pocket. "Maybe you're overlooking something in that photographic memory of yours."

"I tried not to look," I admitted, glancing away. "It's not something I wanted to have seared in my brain." I didn't want to remember his look of disappointment either, preferring the cute smile that reached his eyes instead.

He reached out for me with his free hand and placed it on my arm. "I'm sorry you had to see what you did. But any detail, no matter how small, could help us put together what happened."

"Do you think someone did this to her?"

"It's a possibility we're going to have to look into."

I drew in a long breath, steeling myself, and nodded. "Okay."

For the next several minutes, I recounted everything I remembered, starting with the locked front door.

Finally, it seemed like we were done. "How are you doing?" Grant asked after clicking off the recorder, studying my face for some sort of reaction.

I sighed hard. "Honestly?"

"Yeah, you found a dead body—of someone you know, no less. That's a lot to take in."

And he had no idea that the kitten on his shoulder could literally thank him for bringing him some food. "I have not had nearly enough coffee to deal with this."

"Oh man, I should have thought to offer you something. Water at least. I can call and have someone bring you a drink."

I lifted my hand once more to stop him from saying more. "It's okay. But I should probably get these guys fed. They've been fasting since last night."

"Ugh, I'm really messing this up. Should have let you do that before I got your statement. Sorry, fellas." He reached up and stroked Dodger's head.

"Nah, now they'll be distracted when you have to open the door again. Or do you have to stay here and make sure I don't go anywhere?" Was it weird that I sort of wanted him to?

"If only." His eyes widened and a slight blush appeared on his cheeks. What was that all about—did he also want to stay? "Um, I mean no. Nothing like that. We have officers in both halves of the building now who would prevent that from happening . . . not that your leaving is prohibited at this time."

"Right." That wasn't awkward at all. "Well, thank you for the little bit of company."

"I'm sorry it was under these circumstances." Grant lifted Dodger off his shoulder and gently handed him to me only for the kitten to squirm out of my grasp and down to the floor.

"Me too." But maybe under different ones, it would be better. Not that I was hoping he'd ask to see me again or anything like that. After another moment, I dropped my gaze away from Grant's face—his blush was slowly fading—and to the waiting kittens. "All right, boys, let's get you guys fed."

With the kittens distracted as I tore open the trial-size bag of food, Grant slipped out of the room and back into a potential murder investigation.

chapter
eight

For several minutes, the kittens chowed down while I filled up a bowl of water for them, prepared a litter pan, and straightened the towel in their carrier in case they wanted to curl up and rest in there for a while once they were done eating. No telling how long we were going to be here.

"I liked him," Dodger said between bites.

"Yeah, I did too," I admitted, grateful Dodger hadn't verbally made his opinion known while Grant was here. "Thank you for not saying anything."

"You told me not to. Though I don't understand why. You're talking to me. And you talk to Alphie. So why not him?"

I tried my best to explain it to him, not for the first time. Who knows how well he listened any other time. Familiar or not, he was still a cat. "So because most cats can't talk"—or maybe chose not to, even to us witches—"the average person wouldn't know what to think of one who could. For them, it's make-believe, something out of movies and TV shows. Usually for kids. It's not safe."

"Oh. Okay," he said, disappointed. "He just seemed like something else, that's all."

"Something else as in you could be his familiar?" Grant wasn't in the Snowhaven Coven, though that didn't mean he wasn't a witch. The Moonshadow Coven was based out of Heartwood Hollow only a half hour away from here. His being a solitary witch was also an option. Or maybe his coven was virtual.

"I don't know. What does someone being my familiar feel like?"

"You'll have to talk to Alphie about that." I was curious about the answer too. But since he was entertaining the girls back home—or likely the opposite, that he was being entertained by them—we'd have to wait. In the meantime, I had to update Gemma on the latest feline familiar.

Several new texts from Gemma waited for me. Not surprising given the half-finished text I'd sent when Grant walked in.

> **GEMMA**
> Don't leave me hanging!
>
> That's it? There's gotta be more than that!
>
> I gotta go back to work. There better be a text waiting for me on my break.
>
> **ME**
> Sorry! Had to give a witness statement. I'll fill you in on that and the early talker whenever they let me out of here. I need a coffee stat.

She didn't respond right away, but I would bet money she hid her phone somewhere easily accessible so she'd hear it the moment I responded.

A loud bang on the public-facing door sent the kittens skittering.

"Miss Percy?" Officer Duvall's rough voice called a moment later after a second bang. Was that supposed to be a knock?

"What is it?"

"Your presence is requested at the front desk."

What now? "I already gave my statement."

"That's not what this is about."

I swallowed a lump in my throat. There weren't cameras in here, were there? I didn't think so. But what if there were? What if that was how Dr. Loomis had discovered the truth about familiars? I peeked around the room but didn't see anything. That didn't mean there wasn't. Great. Now I was going to be paranoid that they had captured me not only with a talking kitten but also handling stolen evidence.

"Miss Percy?"

"Coming!" I topped off the small dishes of cat crunchies to send the boys back to their food and hopefully to keep them distracted while I left. Then with a quick "Be good" to the three of them, I snuck out of the room.

The moment I saw Dr. Barker and Tabby waiting for me behind the front desk, I relaxed. They certainly wouldn't still be here if this were about what I'd hidden in my back pocket.

Dr. Barker gave me a concerned but friendly smile as she saw me approach, Officer Duvall close behind me. "How are you holding up?"

"Okay, all things considered. How about you?"

"This is just terrible what happened," she said with a sniff. Her eyes glistened with unshed tears. "And the ripple effects are only getting wider."

"What do you mean?"

She shot a look over to Officer Duvall. "Between this being an active crime scene and the death of Dr. Loomis, we can't be open today. Likely not tomorrow either. We're only here because we got in before they locked the scene down. They've turned other staff away. Patients will start to arrive soon, and we need all the help we can get to call them all."

As if to prove her point, a car pulled into one of the front parking spaces. A moment later, a woman and her dog approached the door. Officer Duvall stepped out to meet them.

Dr. Barker groaned. "And that officer has no bedside manner. He can't be the one to tell everyone that we're closed today." She wasn't wrong there. Thank goodness Grant had interviewed me and not him.

"So we need your help," she continued as Officer Duvall strode back into the building, the woman now getting back into her car. "Would you mind helping Tabby with those phone calls?"

I was more of a texter than a caller, but I could put my preferences aside for this. "Sure, just tell me what to say."

After putting a note on the front door for any client who we couldn't reach in time to express our apologies for the abrupt closure, Tabby and I stayed glued to the phones all morning, calling customers in order of their appointments.

My phone rang, and I glanced at it. It was the animal hospital.

"Tabby, you can hang up now." At her funny look, I held up my cell, showing her the display.

"Oh good Goddess. I wasn't even paying attention. Just going down the line." She hung up the phone. "We should probably get you rebooked, though." With a few clicks of a button, I had a new appointment for the boys lined up for next week.

Outside of Tabby's calling me, the script stayed pretty much the same throughout all of our client calls. "Hi, I'm Nora, calling from the Familiar Friends Animal Hospital. Sorry for the late notice, but due to a building emergency, the office will be closed today and for the rest of the week." From there, the script went in one of a few directions. "We're happy to rebook you for our next available spot starting as early as next Monday." Or "If your pet needs immediate assistance, we have the phone numbers for other practices in town who would be happy to help you."

It took hours, but finally by lunch not only was the front half of the animal hospital cleared from being a crime scene but Tabby and I had reached all but a few customers. We'd left messages, but Tabby would continue calling them. There was nothing left for me to do.

"Why don't you go home?" Dr. Barker suggested as she made her way to the desk, escorted from her office in back by a police officer. She, too, had been glued to a phone for much of the morning. First to tell the staff who hadn't already shown up to not come in and to pass along the news of Dr. Loomis's death. Then, no doubt, to coven leadership to apprise them of the situation.

"Only to drop off the boys. I still have work at the café."

"You've missed over half your shift there. I'm sure they'd understand if you don't go in for the last hour or two. Besides, you worked here. Don't think that won't be compensated. Snowhaven is already aware of the work you've done here today."

"Thank you." Although I didn't have many expenses, and

living in coven-owned housing kept my rent steady and reasonable, missing a shift was never good for my wallet. "That helps."

She put a hand on my shoulder and waited until I made eye contact. "I'd urge you to take whatever time you need off to process what happened. I know you weren't close to Ingrid, I mean, Dr. Loomis, but this can't have been easy for you."

"Thank you. Are you going to take time off too? She was your coworker, and your student before that."

"We'll be closed the next couple of days, and we'll see after that. I'm sure others might need to as well."

I nodded, still contemplating if I should tell her about the small notebook I'd found. But as much as she worked here and knew about the foster familiar program, she wasn't a part of its management. Maybe had Tabby not been staring at us, I would have, but she was a known gossip. This wasn't the sort of information I wanted to have spread around.

One thing still worried me, though. "Do we have cameras here?"

"Cameras?" Dr. Barker seemed confused.

"Yeah, security cameras. Maybe they can show what happened to Dr. Loomis."

Understanding settled across her face. "Ah yes, one's outside and another is pointed at the pharmacy." But thankfully not where I'd found Dr. Loomis and taken the notebook.

"And the one here." Tabby pointed at a spot in the ceiling, where a small dome no larger than a quarter hung affixed to the tile.

"Right. That one too," Dr. Barker said. "Any pertinent footage will be forwarded to the authorities from the security company."

"We hire out for that?" Surprising.

"It's a firm that I'm sure understands the unique nature of what we do here."

"They do," Tabby replied. "Not coven run, but they do a lot of work for various magical clients. And they themselves are too. Magical, I mean."

Dr. Barker raised an eyebrow at her.

"I was here the day they installed it. Chatted with the tech a bit as he put it in." She shrugged as if to show it was no big deal, but the blush creeping up her cheeks told me chatting was likely not all they'd done. She was a big flirt too. "He told me."

"Yes, well, they'll screen the footage and scrub it of anything we can't have regular humans seeing, I'm sure."

"So nothing in the exam rooms?"

"Goodness, no. The rooms are private. Why would you think that?"

"I could see it for insurance purposes, I guess. Was curious, that's all." And relieved that no one would see me flipping through that notebook. "Anyway, I should get the kittens packed up and ready to go. Call me if you need anything here, okay?" I glanced first at Tabby and then to Dr. Barker, who gave me the same concerned, sad smile that she had before.

"And you do the same."

I headed back toward the exam room, eager to get the boys and go home.

But when I opened the door, Grant was inside with Dodger in his lap chattering away.

chapter
nine

"What in the world is going on?" I asked, stepping inside and quickly closing the door, my eyes wide with the implications of this. "Dodger, what did I tell you earlier?"

He rolled off Grant's lap to face me. "You said not to talk to anyone who was dressed like the man who brought us into this room. He isn't."

"I'm pretty sure I said especially not to someone dressed like an officer. You weren't supposed to talk to anyone, period." My gaze flashed to Grant. "What are you doing back in here?"

He stood and raised his hands as if he was going to calm a wild animal. Truthfully, that's a little how I was feeling. My heart raced with fear over messing up my biggest job as a foster—protecting the familiars and hiding the truth of their ability to talk. There went not only my job at the cat café, but potentially one as a vet—certainly here, but how could I be expected to take classes with Dr. Barker after this to even graduate?—and my apartment. They'd kick me out of the coven for sure over this.

One arm still raised in a calm-down fashion, Grant leaned

toward the counter and with the other hand, reached for a to-go cup. "I came to bring you coffee."

"You got me coffee?"

Coffee cup in hand, he straightened and held it out for me. "Yeah. You said you hadn't had enough, so, here."

"Um, thank you." I took the cup from him. Given what had just happened, this still wouldn't be enough, but it was a start. And very sweet of him.

"And I also wanted to say goodbye and give you my card in case you think of anything else that might help us. We've wrapped up our work in the back and are releasing the scene back to the animal hospital."

"Oh. That's good. But how are you not freaking out? About the kitten, I mean."

"Part of the job is to react calmly to the situations that present themselves. I can't let the things I've seen get to me. And I've seen a lot."

I was sure he had. More than one crime scene was enough for me, but "Even talking kittens?"

"You'd be surprised."

I took a sip of the coffee in my hand to keep myself from saying something I shouldn't. Not bad, but not Feline Familiar good either.

"But maybe it would help if you knew more about me," Grant continued. "I don't just work for the Snowhaven PD. I also work for the Supernatural Investigative Service Squad based here in Fiddlefern Fjord."

I took another sip of coffee to stop more words from coming out. Or more specifically, to give better words the chance to form and let those out instead.

"Have you not heard of it?" he asked.

I shook my head.

"But aren't you part of the Snowhaven Coven? If you're fostering familiars, I assumed . . ."

"I am, but I work at the cat café. It's not like I'm in a leadership position. I've never heard of your organization before. What does it do?"

"That would probably take more time than I have right now to explain, but if you're really curious, maybe some other time?"

I didn't miss the slight hue to his cheeks, and despite everything, seeing him again was something I wanted. I cracked a smile at him. "Sure. I'd like that."

"Then let me give you my card." Seemingly out of nowhere, he produced a business card and a pen, which he used to write something on the back. "That's my direct line," he said, tapping on the number when he handed me the card.

I stared at the card for a moment, letting the numbers sink into my memory as I pulled up the contact list in my head and then transferred them to the newest entry for Grant, the cute and familiar-friendly crime scene tech. Who brought me coffee. And might have been asking me out.

I slid the card into my back pocket and smiled. "Thank you."

Grant rubbed the back of his neck. "I have to get going, but I look forward to seeing you again." Then he looked pointedly at Dodger, "And listen to her next time. Don't talk to just anybody. You're lucky it was me. But for the record, I'm glad you did." He glanced up at me and winked, and with that, he ducked out of the room.

"So how exactly did you end up talking to Grant?" I asked Dodger once we were back in the car on the way home.

"I sneezed."

"You sneezed?"

"Into the water. It got up my nose. He said bless you. You've said it to Alphie, and that's what he said back, and Alphie's said bless you to you before, and same thing. You say thank you back. I wasn't thinking. It came out on its own."

I sighed. "Well, at least you're polite."

"I'm sorry."

"It's all right. Just please don't do it again. Can't have you saying thank you to people in the cat café. All it would take is one wrong person and the truth about what we do there—the truth about familiars—would get out." I thought of the notebook still tucked into my back pocket. Could that be why someone killed Dr. Loomis? To protect our secret? But that would mean someone from the coven did it. If someone did it. Maybe she wasn't killed at all. Maybe it was all a terrible accident.

"But Grant was the right person?" Dodger asked, sounding a little worried.

I couldn't have prevented the small smile from creeping onto my face if I'd tried as I pictured Grant winking at me. I'd seen a lot of customers flirting over my few years at the cat café. But not him. He'd never done that before to me or to anyone else there. That had to mean something. So was he flirting? Or was he just trying to lighten up the situation after everything that happened? He had said he was glad Dodger talked. And maybe I was too. It gave me one more person to talk to about all of this. Not that it would actually happen. I didn't have much time to see people outside of work and school. He probably didn't either. But under different circumstances, "Yeah, Dodge. I guess you could say that."

I couldn't see his reaction, but he seemed to settle after my answer. All three boys had, making for a quiet rest of the ride home.

chapter
ten

Alphie was waiting by the door as I walked inside with the boys, Tilly was right behind him, practically on his tail as if she'd not realized he'd stopped and she'd taken an additional step.

"You're home early." He studied me as I closed the door behind me and set the carrier down. "What happened?"

I opened the carrier door, and the boys piled out. Batley and Sport ran past Alphie and Tilly. Dodger did too, but not before saying, "Someone killed the vet."

Alphie's head whipped toward me. "He would be the first to talk. Now, what's this about the vet? Which one?"

"Dr. Loomis."

"Oh." He seemed unconcerned.

"Why do you say it like that?" I hurried to my cabinet for a mug.

"Maybe it's better for all of us that she's not there."

I hadn't been expecting that. My eyes widened. "What do you mean? Because she wasn't a witch? What does that matter? She was a great vet. She certainly didn't deserve to die."

Alphie jumped onto the counter beside where I was prep-

ping a pot of coffee. "No, you're right. That is horrible. It's just—I never liked the way she looked at me."

"But we didn't use her as your vet."

"There was that time Dr. Barker was sick. And then she mistakenly came into the exam room that other time, saw it was us, and then left."

I pressed the button on the pot to start its magic. "Why didn't you say anything?"

"I didn't want to complicate things further. I know you two didn't get along."

Had that been a part of it? That I'd subconsciously picked up on her attitude toward my cat and it affected our interactions with one another? No, not my cat. My familiar.

"She had notes on you."

"On me?"

"Yeah." As the coffee brewed, I told him about the notebook I'd found in her pocket. "I'd have to look again, but I'm sure a lot of the other notes in there were for other familiars."

Tilly jumped onto the counter, landing on Alphie's tail. "Was my name in there?"

Good thing I wasn't already drinking my coffee. Otherwise, Alphie would have been wearing some as I sputtered, "You talk too?"

"Uh-huh," she said proudly.

I shot a look at Alphie. "No wonder you weren't surprised when Dodger told you the news."

"Well, not about him talking, no." He lifted a paw and licked it before rubbing it on his nose. "Plus, what he told me was a bit more surprising, wouldn't you say? We expected some of the kittens to talk. It was just a matter of when."

"Good point." I looked at Tilly. "And I don't know. I haven't finished looking through it."

Done with his face bath, Alphie put his paw down. "You brought it here?"

"What was I supposed to do?"

"Give it to the police?"

"And tell them I contaminated a crime scene?"

He seemed to consider this a moment. "One of the other vets, then."

"I didn't get a chance to." Not that doing so seemed like the right option either. Dr. Loomis was their colleague and friend. As much as it seemed that I was right to not like her, I didn't want to tarnish her memory for them. What good would it have done? But showing it to Grant? That possibility was still an option.

A stream of coffee poured into my *I'm a Witch Before I've Had My Coffee* mug. Of course, I was a witch after having my coffee, too, but at least I was a caffeinated one. It had been my gift in the secret elf holiday exchange at work. Punny mugs were my thing.

"Well, let's have a look," Alphie said as I doctored my coffee. One sugar and a splash of half and half. I saved the fancy drinks for work. I got one free one a day, not that I limited myself to only that one some days, but it saved me from having to buy the supplies and ingredients for my apartment.

"I should head to work after I drink this." I glanced at the digital clock on my coffee pot. "If I leave soon, I could get an hour and a half in."

"If you really want to do that and be the center of attention the whole time, I won't stop you, but we can flip through a few pages before you go."

"Yeah, we can help," Tilly added, unsurprising since even before she could talk, she seemed like she was always backing Alphie up.

I took a sip of my coffee. "All right. It probably would be a good idea to look at the rest of it before I go."

"Yay!" Tilly cheered as she launched herself onto the floor. "Come on, Alphie."

"Kids," he muttered, almost shaking his head as he ambled off the counter. But as much as he protested, I knew he loved the attention.

I followed them to my recliner and placed my mug into the built-in cup holder—the entire reason I picked out this particular style—then sat cross-legged in it. If it were a normal day, I'd raise the leg portion into position, giving the room to whoever wanted it, but then I'd be stuck there for a while. As it was, it would be hard enough to extract myself from the spot as Alphie and Tilly settled between my legs. Even with them positioned so they could see the notebook, it was a pile of fluff as one black and white cat ended and another began.

"What's that symbol?" Tilly asked after several minutes of looking at the notebook. "It was on some of the other pages too."

"It's the symbol for the Snowcraft coven," I explained, tracing the elements. "A large snowflake rising over the hilly landscape. The town uses something similar to this for its logo, too, as do several witch-owned businesses here. Not all of them, though." Unsurprisingly, Feline Familiar's logo was cat and coffee themed.

I looked at the name next to the symbol. "Rascal Hills. That's Gemma's familiar." His full name was Rathskeller, named for the restaurant where the rescue had found him, but as a country music fan, Gemma was thrilled he'd agreed to the nickname to play on the Hills being the opposite of Flatts.

I lifted off the recliner slightly to grab my cell phone from my back pocket, then pressed the buttons on each side to quickly launch the camera app.

"What are you doing?" Alphie asked.

"Taking a picture. Gemma should see this." The entry was little more than Rascal's name, followed by Gemma's, a description of him, and then several numbers. Maybe dates? I flipped back to the beginning. "They're all familiars. Or were suspected to be at one point. See how this one has the coven symbol crossed out?"

"What's that symbol?" Tilly asked as I flipped to another page.

A tree with some shading underneath it. "Maybe a different coven? Moonshadow perhaps." If someone was drawing it quickly and left out much of the detail. "And not all cats either," I added as I turned to the next page, where the letters NEWF appeared. "This is an abbreviation for a Newfoundland, a type of big black dog."

"So she was, what, watching us all to get proof that we were familiars?" Tilly asked as I continued through the notebook and landed on the page with her name. I hadn't gotten this far before.

The next page had Katie's name on it. The one after that, Whisk's. All were followed by my last name. And the numbers were all the same, except the boys had one more than the girls did. I looked at them more closely. "They're dates." I pointed to the last number on Dodger's page. "This is today. And this first number is when you all had your first checkup the day I got you."

I flipped back toward the beginning, where Alphie's name was listed.

"I'm in there too?" He sounded incredulous. "I've never slipped at the vet's, not once."

"She probably suspected you just because of me. See? She's missing your most recent checkup. But this was when Dr. Barker was sick. And this must have been the day she mistakenly popped her head into the exam room, though I wonder now if it really was a mistake."

"Or a way to spy on us."

"It's certainly a possibility." Gemma's warning to me about preventing the kittens from talking to non-witches rang through my head. "It's for their safety. For all our safety, really." And if someone else found out about this, there's no telling what they'd do to keep this sort of information from getting out.

And given what had happened to Dr. Loomis, murder definitely seemed possible.

chapter
eleven

Between studying the notebook and more of the kittens piling on top of me, I couldn't find the oomph to go to work for the last hour of my shift. Besides, one really shouldn't move a cat who is sleeping on them. It's pretty much a universal truth. We'd had several customers at the café over the years find the cat for them—both witches and non-witches alike—by following this rule.

Admittedly, the deciding factor was receiving a text from Gemma while I contemplated which cat I'd disturb first. She assured me it wasn't necessary to come in. They'd asked someone to cover my shift hours ago, so they weren't down a worker, and all anyone could talk about was Dr. Loomis's death. Although not everyone on staff was involved with the animal rescue portion of Feline Familiar, they all knew Dr. Loomis from her frequent visits as a vet to check on a cat when needed and as a customer. The combination of cats and coffee was hard for anyone to resist. Not to mention our soups, sandwiches, and selection of playable board games.

Now I wondered if Dr. Loomis was coming in for more

nefarious reasons. Like trying to figure out which of our adoptable cats could be witch's familiars.

Gemma was waiting for me in the parking lot the next morning as I arrived for my shift and greeted me with a big hug. "How are you holding up?"

"It's been a really strange twenty-four hours."

She let go enough to pull back and study my face with a sympathetic smile. "I can't even imagine finding someone like that, let alone someone you know. Poor Dr. Loomis. She was such a good vet."

"Yeah. About that."

Her look turned quizzical.

"I have something to show you on break."

She dropped her hold on me, and we began our walk to the café. "Why can't you show me now?"

"Because you're going to have questions, and you know how the morning rush is."

"You're worrying me."

I wished I had the right thing to say, that I could tell her there was no need to worry, but I truly didn't know if we should be worried. Dr. Loomis had notes on our familiars and many more. Who knew if this was her only notebook. I momentarily wondered if there was any way for me to find out, but the thought was short lived as we'd reached the café's back door.

"I promise I'll tell you what I know on break," I said as I pulled the door open.

Our coworker Vicki stood a few feet away at her cubby, putting on her apron over the rest of her uniform. Beyond her, the back half of the café already bustled with activity. The front half wasn't open yet, but the kitchen staff had been here for a few hours already prepping the day's fare.

The scent of freshly baked bread and bagels mixed with that of cinnamon and banana from our loaf cakes. Once we were open, the cooks would switch to soups, making sure whatever three we were serving today would be hot and ready come lunchtime, and those smells would take over back here. The coffee smell always hung in the air, but it would be a few more minutes before it would be refreshed as Gemma and Vicki set to brewing the standard pots and getting the fancier machines ready to handle whatever orders came our way.

I made my way *sans* apron to the animal care section of the café. It consisted of two small spaces. The first was an exam room we used for pre-adoption wellness checks and to care for minor issues that didn't need a certified vet to respond to. The second was our storage area. A converted utility closet, it had a water supply for me to fill up bowls, shelving for the bags of dry and wet food, and bins of donated toys and bedding. There were also boards of wood used to repair the raised walkways in the catio and sometimes the cat tree platforms. It was rare for me to need that, though. The most common catio repair I had to make was tightening a few screws here and there, but that was nothing my multi-tool keychain couldn't handle. I took that thing everywhere.

But by far, my favorite element in the room was the new rolling cart that allowed me to wheel in more bowls of food and water than I could carry on my own and prevented me from having to heave thirty-pound bags of kibble and multiple gallon jugs of water into the catio, requiring multiple supply trips and more time. Now, I got to spend the time I saved because of the cart with the cats, a benefit to us all.

"Good morning, everyone," I singsonged a few minutes later as I bumped the catio door open, allowing me to pull the full cart into the room while being better positioned to block any quick escape attempts, not that they tried.

In here, the smells of the café faded away, but the cat smells didn't overpower. I'm sure our customers appreciated that. Sunlight streamed in on two sides from the sizable glass windows extending from waist height on both exterior walls, a large walkway running along their length where the wall met the window. Perfect for stretching out and enjoying the light. Nor was the sunlight overpowering because of the building's orientation, so the room was warm but comfortable, with plenty of shady pockets for those who didn't constantly crave sunny patches at naptime.

No one was sleeping right now, though. The two dozen cats and familiars swarmed the cart, some already chatting away. Amidst meows were:

"Good morning, Nora!"

"I'm so glad to see you!"

"Oh, yay, breakfast!"

"About time. I'm hungry."

And "Where were you yesterday? You said the other day that we'd see you tomorrow, but late, and then you weren't here at all."

I reached down for the silvery-gray cat's head and gave her a soft scratch behind her ears. "Sorry about that. Completely unexpected and unavoidable, I'm afraid."

"Did everything go okay with the kittens?"

They cleared a path for me so I could maneuver the cart to the various feeding stations around the room. As I swapped out empty food bowls for full and old water for fresh, I told them about what happened. They all knew Dr. Loomis. Although we tried to prevent her from doing anything with the familiars once we knew what they were or with the kittens past a certain age when they didn't know any better, she was the vet for most of the non-witchy cats. Not that they had any reaction to the news. After all, I didn't speak cat, just familiar.

"She rubbed me the wrong way," the gray cat, Sylvie, told me. "And I don't mean my fur."

"She watched us a lot," a tuxedo named Audrey added.

I straightened one of the cat beds set into a cubby. "They always said she was good with cats."

"And she was. If you got close enough, which we didn't." Sylvie's gaze darted over to some of the nonfamiliars munching away at their bowls. "But there are always more cats than laps, and she was happy to pet anyone who went over."

"Did she ever have a notebook with her?" I spaced my hands out the size of the small one I'd found.

The familiars all thought a moment before shaking their heads.

"No, but sometimes she took photos," Audrey said.

But who didn't when they came here? I would have found it stranger if she hadn't. Taking photos and sharing them on social media was openly encouraged here. The more eyes on everyone who needed homes, the better. In my head, snippets of memories played out before me of people with their phones out and pointing them in various directions and angles, trying to get pictures of the cats, sometimes of themselves with the cats too. This included Dr. Loomis, who always took a spot on the floor despite all the chairs in here. Also not that unusual.

"Thanks. If any of you think of something else, please let me know."

I joined Gemma and Vicki behind the counter once I was done with my morning catio chores. After my break, there'd be another round to check on everyone in there and once more before I left. Someone else on staff would handle the evening feed and make one final round before the café closed for the night. Because of the gaming section in the back of the café, our hours extended later than most others in the area, and often became the home for one-shot tabletop RPGs or small board game tournaments between friends or a quick stop for caffeine before Barkade—a bar and 21+ arcade—opened for the night two doors down on the other side of Dawg Pound, a quasi-fast-food joint that served hot dogs with all sorts of toppings.

Vicki slid a large coffee my way, the foamed milk gently cresting the top of the unlidded cup. "You're always so good with them. It's like they're actually having a conversation with you."

"Eh, you just have to know how to talk to them, that's all," I joked.

Over her shoulder, Gemma gave me a look as if she couldn't believe I went there. Protecting the familiars was important, especially now, but I needed to blow off some steam after all that had happened. Besides, Vicki didn't know about the familiars among the rest of the cats. All I was doing was cementing myself in her mind as a future stereotypical cat lady. If she didn't think I was one already.

I glanced away from Gemma as my lips curled into a smile, careful not to make eye contact with her again or else I'd laugh, which wouldn't make her any happier with me. Coffee time. Cappuccino or latte based on the foam. The weight as I lifted the cup said latte. I blew across the top, rippling the foam, before taking a sip. The rose scent hit me as the floral notes skated over my tastebuds dueting with some earthy spice I couldn't figure out. Vicki wasn't a witch, but her brews were magical. "What is this? Besides delicious, of course."

She grinned proudly. "Rose and cardamom latte. A regular shot of espresso, steamed milk, and foam, along with our rose syrup. A pinch of cardamom as you pour the syrup and another on top is all you need to round it out."

"I really like it. This is going to be wicked popular today." I had another taste. "So good. I could just stand here all morning with this."

Gemma shot me another look, this time of the *please, don't* variety as she scooted around Vicki and me toward the door that led into the kitchen while Vicki, unable to see said look, replied, "I don't think anyone would blame you after what happened yesterday."

"Thanks, though I promise I won't."

"Good," Gemma said as she came back into the room pulling one cart full of baked goods as Amy followed her pushing another, "because today promises to be a busy day."

I took one long swig of my latte before stowing it under the counter, next to where Gemma and Vicki had placed theirs, and followed Gemma to the counter where we'd prep for the grab-and-go case while Amy stocked shelves for our dining-in orders.

Gemma slid a banana loaf onto the counter in front of her, then handed me a roll of plastic wrap so I could work on packing the slices she cut. "And don't think I've forgotten what you need to show me either."

chapter
twelve

Gemma followed me to the staff entrance during our mid-morning break between the late breakfast and early lunch crowds. I grabbed my phone out of my bag. There was a text message from Dr. Barker in my notifications.

> Funeral for Dr. Loomis on Sunday. 1:00 at Winters's.

As I pulled up the photo gallery, I updated Gemma on the text and made plans to meet at the funeral home where the services were being held.

Then I sat next to her on the bench running in front of the row of cubbies and silently handed her the phone. Would she come to the same conclusions I had without being told?

She studied it a moment. "What is this? A notebook?" When I nodded, she followed up with, "Whose handwriting is this?"

"Dr. Loomis's."

"Why is Rascal's name written down? She wasn't his vet."

"It's a good question. The fosters were all in there, but she was treating them. But Alphie's was too."

"And he doesn't see Loomis either."

"Not usually. Only the one time Barker was sick. But that was noted in there as well. What else do you notice?"

She moved her fingers apart on the screen, zooming in on the image. "Those are dates," she said, coming to that conclusion sooner than I had. She pointed at the last set of numbers. "I just took him in two weeks ago. But we didn't see her. So how did she know that?"

I explained how she'd "accidentally" popped into the exam room one time when Alphie and I were there.

"She didn't do that with us. At least not then."

"She's done it before?"

"Yeah. I always thought it was to say hi because she knows me. That she remembered Rascal from when he was a kitten and wanted to see the huge fluff he'd turned into after being so scrawny." She shifted the image to see more while still zoomed in. "These are all our visits for the last two years. I'm sure of it."

Had she been onto us for that long? "She was just out of vet school then. She graduated the spring before I started."

"Guess you'll be getting that job sooner rather than later."

I shook my head. "Not until I'm certified. I can't even take the exam for another year and a half."

She brightened. "Right. Stuck with me for a little longer, then."

"Pssh, between the animal rescue and my need for good caffeine, you know I'll be stuck with you even after."

She shoved me playfully before hitting the screen with her index finger. "That's the Snowhaven Coven logo."

"It's not the only one in there either. Moonshadow and another I'm not familiar with."

"So what, she was keeping track of our cats?"

"Not our cats." There was a dog, too, but that was beside the point. "Our *familiars*."

Recognition slowly dawned across her face. "But she's not a witch."

"I know."

"She's not supposed to know about them," she said in a rush, clearly getting anxious.

"I know."

"How did she find out?"

"I don't know."

"Wait. How do you know as much as you do?" She held up the phone. "How do you have this?"

"I took it from Dr. Loomis after I found her."

"You what?!" she whisper-shouted.

"I saw Dodger's name on the page it was open to, and I panicked!"

She stuck out her lower lip and blew hard, the puff of air lifting a small portion of her bangs. "Wow."

I leaned back against the row of cubbies and found myself saying "I know" once more. "I stole evidence."

"No, you did the right thing. You protected the familiars. That's our number one priority. No telling what would have happened had the police figured it out."

"What do I do now?"

"Give it to the other vet. Or one of the coven's priestesses." But that didn't sit right with me. "Why are you making that face?"

"What if someone else already knew about this notebook? Or if not about the notebook, then that she was aware of the familiars? What if this is why she's dead?"

"You think someone"—she lowered her voice to a whisper—"killed her over this?"

"I don't know for sure, but you said it yourself. It's certainly an extreme way to go about it, but protecting the familiars is a top priority."

"Oh good Goddess. So are you just going to hold on to it then?"

"I'm not sure." I thought of the business card Grant handed me before he left, its image appearing in my mind, along with that of the crime scene tech himself. As if it were right in front of me, I flipped the imaginary business card over. His phone number scrawled on the surface, lifted off the card and floated above imaginary Grant's handsome face.

"Okay, you just smiled. Where did your mind go? It certainly wasn't about this."

I was going to tell her about Grant when Amy passed by the hallway pushing a cart with three large soup pots on it. Our signal that break was over and it was time to shift the café's offerings to lunch.

"Later," I assured her as the business card and phone number disappeared from my mind's eye while Grant's image lingered a little longer and slowly faded as I made my way back to the front end of the café.

chapter
thirteen

When Grant came into the café shortly after the lunch rush, I momentarily had to wonder if he was here or if I was imagining him again. But I'd not seen him in this outfit before, so here he was. He caught my eye and smiled. Stuck behind the counter with a short line in front of me, I nodded to acknowledge him, but he'd have to wait his turn otherwise.

"You got a few minutes?" he asked after placing his order with me.

Maybe he had some information about Dr. Loomis. I glanced at the clock on the wall. "My break starts in fifteen."

"Perfect. I'll start in on my coffee while I wait for you."

His peanut butter cup latte sounded good, and with my break coming up, I was due for another coffee. I keyed a second one into the register, and as I took the next customer's order, Vicki got started on mine and Grant's drinks. When she was done, she called out Grant's name so he could get his and slipped mine under the countertop for me.

Several minutes later, I pulled off my apron and put it up on a hook by the counter where I'd grab it after break. Then I took my coffee and met Grant at one of the small tables toward the back of the room.

"Don't sit," he said as I placed my hand on the chair across from him. He didn't say it meanly, but it gave me pause all the same. As if picking up on my hesitation, he smiled reassuringly. "Is there somewhere more private we can go?"

I thought for a moment. The best place would have been the small exam room I used for pre-adoption checks, but I couldn't take a customer into the back without them being in the process of adopting a cat. I glanced toward the catio. Someone was just leaving. I ticked my head to the wall separating this space from that one. "They'll see us in there, but they won't be able to hear us."

"Good enough." He stood, and we made our way into the catio.

When the door closed, I introduced him to the cats and familiars. "He knows about you all, so it's okay to talk if you need to. But remember, that this is a onetime exception to my usual rule."

"Only one time?" Grant asked, humor lacing the question. "Darn. You know how often I'm already here. Might be nice to have company sometimes when I come. Beyond just the feline kind."

Heat crept slowly up my neck, and I hoped it wasn't obvious.

"Did you bring us any treats?" Sylvie asked him.

"Not today, I'm afraid. But maybe next time if Nora allows it."

Everyone turned to look at me, even the cats. They didn't need to be familiars and know how to talk to know what we were talking about. The word *treat* was universally understood.

"We'll see," I said, promising no more than that. I pulled a cat bed off of two chairs set up next to one another and sat down, indicating for Grant to do the same. "What did you need to talk about?"

Sylvie was in my lap the moment I lifted my drink to my mouth while I waited for him to speak. Audrey took Grant's lap and two of the cats investigated his shoes as he said, "We've gotten some of the preliminary tests back from Dr. Loomis's autopsy."

"That's fast, isn't it?"

He nodded. "Can be. But given where this happened and who most of you are there, I called in a favor with one of the lab techs at SISS, and I helped run a few myself. Dr. Loomis didn't die of natural causes."

"So you're saying she was murdered?"

"I am. Some sort of poison. We're trying to narrow it down now."

"Do you have any leads?"

He shook his head. "It's still early since we just classified it as a homicide, but our initial investigation isn't turning up much of anything. Good reputation as a vet, seemingly liked by her colleagues and her neighbors, and no signs of any problems with her husband."

I furrowed my brow. "That's not what I'd heard."

"You mean from the receptionist at the animal hospital?" I nodded. "All conjecture on her part. She admitted as much. Detectives allege he's a nice guy. Car mechanic. Appears genuinely distraught over this. I know I already questioned you, but she never said anything to you, did she?"

"I didn't even know she was married until several weeks ago when Tabby brought it up. We weren't close enough for any sort of conversation about people who might not like her."

"Sounds like there was more to it than that."

"Can't say we really got along." I explained Gemma's theory to him, about me being her eventual replacement at the animal hospital.

"So knowing what the kittens could be, why was she scheduled to do the surgery that morning?"

"Familiars aren't supposed to talk that early. We thought it was safe. She took care of a lot of the cats here as well."

"Just not the talking ones," Sylvie added, stretching her paw up onto the armrest of the chair.

"Speaking of, how is my little friend?"

"Good. The boys all go back next week for their surgery."

"Tell him I said hi."

"I will."

Grant drained the rest of his coffee. I'd still barely touched mine, but he'd had a head start. "I should get going. Gotta work this investigation on two ends right now until we have a suspect or a motive. But I wanted to let you know because I'm sure the news will pick up the story."

And the concerned looks I'd been getting from my coworkers would only continue. "I might know one reason . . ."

"Really?"

I took a deep breath. "She had this notebook. In it were a lot of names of familiars. Mine was in there. So was Gemma's. Several of the ones in here now and ones we've already adopted out. Has dates that I believe to be vet visits and coven-related symbols. It's like she was tracking them."

"How do you know this?" One of his eyebrows raised.

I clasped my cup so tightly that it buckled at the top where there wasn't any liquid left to stabilize it. "I took it from her that morning. It was peeking out from under her as if it had fallen out of her pocket when she fell."

Grant lifted his hand to his forehead and slowly drew his index and middle fingers and his thumb together at the center. "So you contaminated a crime scene?"

"It was open, and I saw Dodger's name on it, and I didn't want to disturb the scene even more by putting it back."

He rubbed his hand down his face. "Why didn't you leave it there and tell us what you'd done?"

"And tell people who aren't witches and aren't supposed to know about familiars what everything in that notebook meant? It's my duty as a foster to protect the familiars first and foremost. And that means keeping their secret. Tell me, if it wasn't you who Dodger had sneezed in front of, how do you think that would have gone when he talked?"

He lifted the hand that had been petting Audrey up in surrender. "Point taken. What did you do with the notebook? Do you still have it?"

I nodded.

"Can I see it?"

"I don't have it here. We're not all witches here. It's not something I wanted to keep on me."

"Could we get together sometime soon so you can show it to me?"

"I have a day off in two days. It's Dr. Loomis's funeral that morning. I can meet up with you after that."

"What are your thoughts about baked goods?"

An interesting change of topic, but okay . . . "Our mousse mouse is very popular." I pointed toward the dessert case to the mouse-shaped mousse figures covered in chocolate ganache.

"I meant you personally. Do you like them?"

I cracked a smile. "The mousse mouse is a very popular choice of mine."

"Well, there's a bakery over in Heartwood Hollow I've been

meaning to check out. Run by a kitchen witch who spells the treats. Seemingly unintentionally." His voice softened, and his gaze darted to my eyes and away again. "Want to come with me?"

Why did this sound like it was more than just getting together for me to show him contaminated evidence? Was he asking me on a date? Either way, my answer would have been the same. "That sounds great."

"We can talk about what you found up there while we're at it."

I nodded. Okay, so not a date. But that boyish grin on his face couldn't just be about the notebook. Or about the kitchen witch in Heartwood Hollow. So maybe this *was* sort of a date...

Gemma knocked on the door to the catio and pointed at the clock behind her on the wall, but as she did, she waggled her eyebrows at me. No doubt due to my being in here with Grant. I'd have to explain later.

"Looks like my break is up. Thanks for stopping in to tell me about Dr. Loomis." I gently tapped Sylvie. "Gotta get up, sleepyhead."

She let out a small groan as she slid down to the floor, allowing me to get up. But the moment I put the cat bed that had been there back onto the chair, she hopped into it and curled up.

Audrey did the same once Grant stood and returned the cat bed to that chair. His black pants were covered in white cat fur.

"We have rollers you can use."

"Got one in my car. My cat has some white on him too."

Grant followed me out of the catio. "Thanks for meeting with me. I'll see you in a couple days."

"You're welcome. I'm looking forward to it." I took another sip of my coffee before heading back behind the counter. After I washed my hands and put my apron back on, I turned around to see that Grant was in line again. I couldn't hide the smile on my face.

"Who is the cutie?" Gemma asked as she passed behind me on the way to make a drink for the customer she'd just rung out.

"Not now." I took her place at the register to take care of the next customer.

She prepped the blender for a smoothie, and when the next customer requested one as well, I slid the drink ticket toward her and whispered, "He was at the vet's yesterday. Crime scene tech."

She nodded, then turned on the blender. "But you like him, though."

Hopefully the blender noise blocked anyone else from hearing her say that. Grant was only one person away in line.

"Maybe," I answered before returning to the register. It was more than a little complicated, to say the least, but the flush from earlier warmed my cheeks once more.

"You talked me into it," Grant said as he stepped up to the counter. "A mousse mouse does sound pretty good."

"I promise they're delicious." I rang him up, then placed a mouse into a to-go container before handing it to him. "Here you go."

"Thanks. And for the record, I'm also looking forward to seeing you in a couple days." His boyish grin returned in full force. He winked, and with a "See you then," he walked out of the coffee shop trailed by Gemma's squeal of delight. No doubt this would be all she'd talk about from now until after I saw him again.

chapter
fourteen

O. M. Winters and Sons' Funeral Home was situated in the hillier side of town at the end of Second Street where the tighter-packed homes behind the main streets gave way to those that were spread out with larger yards the farther away from the town center they got. It was about as far as one could get in Snowhaven from the commercial area where the coffee shop and the animal hospital a few blocks away were.

The funeral home itself was old but well-kept and ornate. A Victorian something or other, but I wasn't sure exactly. From what I knew, the sons of O. M. Winters and Sons' now took care of most of the business with the elder O. M. Winters being more of the figurehead. His photographic portrait greeted Gemma and me in the foyer. Two hallways branched out from there, and a man in a black suit asked us who we were there for before sending us down the hall to the right.

Gemma nudged me. "Looks like O. M. Winters wasn't the first." She pointed to the many portraits on the wall with little plaques underneath. Oswald Milo. Otis Michael. Oscar Mitchell. "Surprised they aren't all the same."

I shrugged. "I'm sure some are. Maybe they didn't go into

the business." Including the one in the foyer, there were seven portraits in total. The oldest three were paintings and not photographs.

A line curved into the hallway, forcing us to stop at the second oldest painting, and I hoped it would move quickly. I was meeting Grant after this, not that I'd given him an exact time, but the sooner I could get out of here and see him, the better. Now knowing for sure that Dr. Loomis had been murdered, coupled with his reaction to my having potential evidence, had been weighing on me. Was it really why she had been killed? What if someone had wanted that notebook? What if they still wanted it?

A long-ago O. M. Winters stared disapprovingly at me from his portrait. Judging me. Either for having taken the notebook or for being focused on that when I should be focused on paying my respects. Fortunately, we soon moved ahead by several spots in line, stopping us in front of the last portrait. Oliver Monroe. He had kinder eyes. Less judgy. Like he'd understand my not being present in the moment.

Finally, after a few more minutes, we made it inside the large room, and there were no O. M. Winters portraits to be seen. Instead, a slideshow of photographs from Dr. Loomis's life played on one wall while easels with pictures affixed to poster boards stood for people to look at. We signed the guest registry and continued on our way, perusing the photos as we went.

The last easel held the most recent photos, but even they went back a few years. In one, Dr. Barker and another professor from the veterinary school sat at a dinner table with a younger Dr. Loomis, just Ingrid back then, I assumed, and several other veterinary students. Some I recognized because they were only a year ahead of me, and others I didn't. On the table were a big bowl of salad, several bottles of dressing, and various toppings. Dr. Loomis was laughing about something. I'd never known her this way. Though this was her before the animal hospital, before her finding out about the familiars.

The only time she'd come close to laughing around me was that first exam with the seven kittens when I'd caught her with lettuce in her teeth, before I tried cracking a joke with her and reminded her that we were not on those sorts of terms with one another.

Dr. Barker was several people ahead of us in line, chatting with Tabby and another vet. Tabby noticed me looking and waved politely, a sad smile on her face. The other vet nodded her hello. Dr. Barker must have asked Tabby who she'd seen because Tabby said something, and then Dr. Barker turned around. She mouthed hello, followed by "I need to talk to you."

I pointed at myself and she nodded. I mouthed back okay before she turned back around almost to the receiving line.

What felt like ages later, Gemma and I had finally said our condolences to everyone closest to Dr. Loomis. Grant had been right. Her husband was distraught. Poor guy. But did he know about what she'd discovered? If not, who did?

Dr. Barker was waiting for us, sitting in one of the many folding chairs set up for the service taking place after calling hours ended. Tabby, Morgan, and the other vet and tech were seated next to and behind her, along with several faces I recognized from veterinary school, both staff and former students.

"Saved these for you." Dr. Barker patted the padded metal seat next to her. "Gemma, good to see you again, though something other than these circumstances would have been more preferable. How are you?"

The two exchanged pleasantries as we filed into the row of chairs and sat down, me between Gemma and Dr. Barker.

When they were done, Dr. Barker turned to me. "I have an offer for you, and while I usually wouldn't be discussing such a thing here, it's the reason we're here that I'm able to offer it to you right now at all."

I nodded to let her know I was listening.

"With poor Ingrid gone, the rest of the staff and I are all having to fill in to cover her patient load at least until we find another vet to take her place." She quirked a grin. "Can't really wait the two years for you to graduate, but with us all taking on more, we'll be needing to shift things off of our plates. The techs will pick up some of that, but the council hopes you'll consider swapping some of your café shifts for help at Familiar Friends. What do you say?"

"I'd be honored, thank you. You know that's been my goal all along, to work there."

"Oh, I'm so glad to hear it." Around her, the other staff members smiled and nodded in agreement. "And you'll find that it pays better than the café as well."

"Even better." I'd need that money to pay for the coffee I required but wouldn't be able to get for free like I could when working at the café.

"The hospital is still closed tomorrow, but we'll be resuming normal hours the day after. I'll alert the right people within the council, and someone will let your manager know to drop some of your shifts. We obviously still need you there at least sometimes for when people come to adopt the cats and to check on their general well-being. Gemma can handle some of it, but with her being a year behind you, we don't quite have anyone ready to fill your shoes there."

Dr. Barker and I had always had a good relationship, right

from the moment I started in veterinary school—before that really, ever since I'd started volunteering for the rescue and met her as she provided checkups to the newly adopted cats and familiars. She was someone I looked up to in the coven as well. So it warmed me to hear her say that no one could replace me. I truly loved working at Feline Familiar, and I wasn't ready to leave it completely.

"Thank you again," I said as Dr. Loomis's loved ones took seats in the front row. An elderly gentleman, who could only be O. M. Winters himself, came from somewhere in the back of the room. He placed a hand on the shoulder of Dr. Loomis's mother before quietly exchanging a few words with her.

Still facing the front, Dr. Barker leaned toward me and whispered, "He's Ingrid's uncle."

I didn't know what to say to that beyond a simple oh. The Winters family was among the oldest in town, having been among the founding families of Snowhaven. Those families had been almost equally split among witches and non-witches, though by all accounts, the non-witches had no knowledge of that fact. At least not then. Everyone now knew of the Snowhaven Coven, just like they knew of the many churches in town. The openness of the town was one of several things that had drawn me to it after I left Baycliff when I graduated from college.

It wasn't until after I'd moved here that I learned that, although the witches here were no secret, the truth of any real magic was kept within the coven. And that included the familiars. My magic, if one could even call it that, was one of the rare exceptions. A photographic memory was well within the realm of understanding for everyone. Even the occasional non-witch claimed to have the same.

So why was Dr. Loomis, a member of one of Snowhaven's

non-witch founding families, looking into familiars? How had she found out about them? And what had she been planning to do with that information?

Before I could go down that line of thought, O. M. Winters approached the podium, signaling the start of the service.

When it was over, the veterinary staff, Gemma, and I walked out through a secondary entrance, allowing us to escape the gaze of the hallway portraits. They made plans to have lunch together at a nearby bistro, and I semi-regretfully declined their invitation as they took a head count to call in a reservation. The bistro's take on classic dishes made for delicious food, some of my favorite, but Grant was waiting.

Dr. Barker had just gotten off the phone with the bistro when I saw my car, its passenger-side window smashed open.

"Oh no," I breathed at the same time as Gemma gasped, her hands flying to her mouth.

I raced to my car, Gemma right behind me.

"Oh no, oh no," I repeated.

Inside the car, my glove box sat open, the contents shoved this way and that, some of it strewn onto the passenger seat. Careful of the glass, I reached in, hoping I'd find it, but knowing it was no use.

Dr. Loomis's notebook with all the familiars' names in it was gone.

chapter
fifteen

I reached in through the window to unlock the car and threw the door open.

"Shouldn't you call the police?" Gemma asked. "You're getting your hands all over potential evidence."

Now she was worried about me handling evidence? The irony wasn't lost on me. She'd had no problem with me removing evidence when I told her about it a few days ago. And now that evidence was missing.

I reached under the passenger seat, careful to avoid the glass in the footwell. "They didn't touch the door. They went through the window."

"This is why I leave my car doors unlocked."

"Not helping, Gem," I gritted out, confirming the notebook hadn't slid under the seat and grabbing my purse that I'd stowed under there before heading into the funeral home. I hadn't wanted to carry a bag inside.

"Sorry," she said as the vet staff reached my car.

"Oh no, Nora. I'm sorry," Dr. Barker said sympathetically before she softly asked the group, "Now who would do something like that at a funeral? And why your car?"

The veterinary staff looked around the parking lot, no doubt realizing Dr. Barker was right, that mine was the only car broken into.

I just shrugged. The answer to her second question was easy. Because my car had something whoever did this hoped would be inside. But I couldn't say that. The question of who had two possible answers. Either someone who knew what Dr. Loomis was doing because they were working with her or because they killed her.

After double-checking that my wallet and phone were still inside my purse, I took the latter out. "I'm going to call about my car. You all can go to lunch."

"If you're sure," Dr. Barker said, hesitation lacing her words. "I can call the bistro back and push our reservations to a little later."

I stood. "No need. It's fine."

"Are you going to be okay?" Tabby asked.

"Yeah. It's a pain, but it could have been worse." I tapped my bag for emphasis and hoped I sounded unconcerned.

"I'll stay with her," Gemma said. "We can sit in my car until help arrives."

Gemma and I said our goodbyes to everyone from the vets and walked over to her car a few spots away. As I slid onto her passenger seat, I recalled the number on Grant's business card and plugged them into the phone.

"Aren't you going to call the police?" Gemma asked.

I shook my head. "And say what, that someone stole a notebook I took from a crime scene?"

"Oh," she said quickly before letting out a second oh, this time holding the *O* sound longer as realization spread.

"Yeah. So I'm calling Grant."

"Right, your date is today."

"It's not a date, and it's not happening anymore now that our reason for meeting is probably in a murderer's hands right now."

She gave me a sympathetic smile as I pressed the call button on my screen.

"Hey, Grant, it's Nora," I told him when he answered after the second ring.

"Nora, hi. I'm almost to Heartwood Hollow. Figured I'd head over early to check out the town. It's seen an increase in paranormal activity, so I thought I'd explore it a bit before we meet up at the bakery."

The words came out in a rush. "I'm not going to be able to make it."

"Oh." He sounded disappointed. "Just too drained after the funeral? I know you said you two weren't close, but that sort of thing can happen if you have a higher level of empathy or are an empath. You aren't, are you?"

"No."

"It's not the bakery, is it? We can meet somewhere more convenient if that's better."

"It's not that." Why couldn't I just come out and say it?

"You're not considering not sharing what you know, are you? I'm not going to turn you in or anything because I know how important it is to protect the familiars, but it's still evidence. SISS can handle it."

I took a deep breath and in a rush said, "It's gone, Grant. The notebook."

"What do you mean?"

"Someone busted my window and stole it out of my car while I was at the funeral."

"Is anything else missing?"

"No."

"Then you were targeted. Did anyone else know you had the notebook?"

My gaze darted to Gemma. There was no way she would have done this. And besides, we were both in the funeral home when it happened. "Only my best friend. Her cat was in there too." Had someone at the coffee shop somehow overheard Grant and me? Or me telling Gemma about it? I'd been so careful. "Maybe the killer found out it wasn't taken as evidence? Or maybe someone Dr. Loomis was working with? I don't know who else would have known that it existed."

Grant sighed hard, and I imagined him rubbing his hand down his face like when I first told him I had it. "Okay. It will be okay. Whoever has it has to be involved somehow. We solve this case and we'll get it back."

"You're not mad?" I really had wanted to go to the kitchen witch's bakery with him, but there was no need to go now. He was already on his way there, and why would he go back, especially with me?

"It's not like you planned for your car to get broken into. Did you call the police?"

"You're the first person I called. Didn't want you to think I'd stood you up."

His voice softened. "Call them. You'll need a report of this if you're planning on going through your insurance to get the window fixed. Just don't tell them about the notebook."

"I won't."

"I'm just getting into the town now, so I'm going to let you go, but we'll talk soon."

"Okay. Enjoy the bakery."

"Sorry you couldn't come." He sounded disappointed.

I was too. "Sorry about all of this."

"It will be okay, Nora. We'll get that notebook back. The kittens will be safe."

"Thanks." I needed to hear that more than I'd realized.

We hung up, and I filled Gemma in. "I should double-check to make sure nothing else is missing."

The parking lot had pretty much cleared out by the time I got off the phone with Grant, so there were no cars to maneuver around as I stepped out of her car and walked back over to mine. Gemma's door opened and closed behind me, and then the sound of her footsteps followed.

But those weren't the only ones I heard.

chapter
sixteen

A heavier set of footsteps approached from my side. "Are you okay?" a familiar male voice asked. I wouldn't have recognized it at all had I not given my condolences to him just a short time before.

I turned my head to see Dr. Loomis's widower standing a few feet away, suit jacket now unbuttoned, tie loosened, and face no less sad although now also reflecting concern for me. "Someone busted my window."

"While you were at Ingrid's funeral?" Nodding, I pivoted toward him. "What sort of person does that? I'm sorry."

"Not your fault. I was trying to figure out what got taken before I called the police for my insurance company, but I think it's all here."

He walked closer, surveying the damage. "What type of insurance do you have?"

"It's one of those national chains." I'd picked it because I liked the commercial.

"I mean, do you have a comprehensive policy?"

"Umm..."

"If you don't have a comprehensive policy and nothing got

taken, there's no reason to call them or the police. Insurance won't cover the window without a top-tier policy, and even then, this is probably not more than your deductible, so you're still out money on top of your premium going up. You're better off just paying for the repair."

And then I wouldn't have to cover up what really got stolen. "Thanks. That probably saves me a lot of money."

"Do you have a body shop you go to?"

I shook my head. "Haven't needed work here. Typically take care of car stuff when I visit my parents in Baycliff."

He made a face. "Oof. Little far to be going with a busted window. Tell you what. I recently took over the garage on Flurry off of East Ridge. If you can get it over to the shop, I'll get you what it needs. Give you the friends and family discount."

"I couldn't ask you to do that. You don't know me."

"But you came today. So you knew Ingrid. That's good enough for me."

"I don't think she liked me," I confessed. Why, I wasn't sure. Especially since he was trying to save me money. "It was the right thing to do. She was ahead of me in vet school and took care of some of my foster cats, and I found her."

"Excuse me?"

"I found her. That day. I'm the one who found her and called 911."

Before I could register what was happening, the man's arms were around me. Gemma's eyes widened in surprise, and she took a step forward as if she was going to try to get him off me, but I held a hand up to stop her.

He was hugging me. And because I felt he needed it, I raised my arms to reach around him and hug him back. A sob racked his body. "Thank you."

"I couldn't do anything. It was too late."

"But you didn't leave her."

No, I didn't, but I had taken the notebook from her, and that's what had gotten stolen out of my car, prompting this whole exchange. Not that I was going to tell him that. What a weird circle this had become.

I patted his back. "I'm sorry for your loss."

He sniffed and released his hold on me as he took a step back. "And I'm sorry for losing my composure like that. I wasn't expecting what you said. No one really told me what happened that morning." He dabbed at his eyes with his suit jacket sleeves.

"You don't need to apologize for that. It's been a trying time for you."

"Thank you for understanding. I should go. I'm holding up the rest of the family for a late lunch. But I needed to make sure you were okay. Ingrid would have wanted me to."

He took another step back and gave me a half smile. "I'm serious about coming to the shop. I'll be open bright and early tomorrow . . . need to get some semblance of normalcy back into my life, but you can drop it off anytime. There's a key slot in the door."

I nodded. "Thanks again. I'll bring the car by sometime tomorrow." Wasn't sure how I'd get back across town to get to work, but I'd figure it out.

"Thanks for coming. And thank you for what you did for Ingrid." And with that, he turned and walked away.

Gemma came up beside me. "That was some good timing. I didn't know that about car insurance. I don't know what I have either. Should probably look that up."

"I know I don't have comprehensive. It was more expensive."

"Then I definitely don't have it." She sputtered a laugh before regaining her composure. "I know you said you'd drop it off tomorrow, but why don't we just go and get it over with now? I can follow you and take you back to your place."

"But then I can't get to work in the morning."

She waved a hand at me dismissively. "Sure you can. I'll come get you. It's not like you're far."

Leaving no room for argument, not that I was going to, she turned on her heels and walked away, saying, "Lead the way. I'll follow you."

chapter
seventeen

I'd been back in my apartment after Gemma dropped me off for maybe an hour and a half when a knock at the door sent the cat and kittens scrambling. Some for cover, others toward the door, and still more somewhere in between. I had half a mind to ignore it. This had been quite a day already, and I didn't really want to deal with anyone else. I was still debating answering when whoever it was knocked again.

"Are you going to get that," Alphie asked, "or can we start to crowd your lap again?"

"I should at least go grab a snack before any of you fall asleep on me again and I get stuck. Maybe make more coffee too." I lowered the leg rest, then stood up from my seat.

At that moment, the phone rang, and I grabbed it off the arm of the recliner. The number on the screen wasn't one I had programmed in, but I knew it.

"Hey, Grant."

"I promise it's not a door-to-door salesman outside." A teasing tone played across his words.

My stomach flip-flopped, and despite only having one cup

of coffee since I'd gotten home, I suddenly felt jittery, as if on the verge of over-caffeination. "That was you?"

"Come open the door and find out."

I grabbed my *this witch needs her coffee* mug, then crossed through my kitchen, doing as Grant said. Dodger, who had initially run toward the door at the knocking sound, stayed by my feet while Alphie and Tilly rushed onto the counter where they would have a prime view of . . . whatever was about to happen.

Although I was happy to see him, the feeling was quickly replaced with uncertainty. The jittery sensation tightened into a twisty ball of anxiety. Why was he here? The notebook was gone. Or maybe that was it. He'd come to arrest me for withholding evidence. And besides that, how had he gotten my address? Had they gotten a warrant and now he was luring me out to the police?

Thank goodness for peepholes.

Grant stood alone in the hallway of my apartment building, rocking back and forth from his heels to his toes. And instead of a warrant, he held a large white paper bag in one hand. On it was the name Suncraft Bakery and what appeared to be their logo—a cupcake with its pink-and-yellow frosting rising over the name as if it was the sun.

I placed my coffee mug on the counter, then opened the door, my worry about being arrested disappeared, and the knot that had started to form loosened as the fluttery feeling took over once more.

Grant broke out into a broad grin as we made eye contact. "Hey, Nora. Since you couldn't make it out to the bakery, I figured I'd bring the bakery to you." He lifted the bag to chest height.

I chuckled as I stepped aside so he could come in. "The whole bakery from the looks of it. How much did you get?"

"Well, I wasn't sure what you liked, so I got an assortment." He stepped inside, and I closed the door.

"Hi!" Dodger chirped, lifting onto his hind legs and placing one front paw on Grant's pant leg while the other reached up for him.

"Well, hello again." Grant squatted to pet Dodger, placing the bag on the floor, before picking him up. Dodger wriggled playfully out of his grasp and climbed onto his shoulder, allowing Grant to grab the bag and stand up once more.

I blinked rapidly at the scene before me.

Dodger gave me a slightly guilty look, though it was hard to pull off as he lifted his chin for Grant's fingers. "I know I'm not supposed to talk to people. But he already knew, so that's okay, right?"

"Yeah, that's fine. But really? You let him pick you up just like that?" To Grant, I added, "He doesn't do that for me."

"He's my buddy," Grant replied, holding the bag toward me. "We had a good conversation waiting for you at the vet's."

I took it from him, swinging it past my familiar and Tilly, both of them following the motion with their whole bodies as I placed it on the counter a few feet away from them.

Rooted in place, Alphie stretched as far as he could toward the bag, lifting a paw toward it. "There's more in that bag than just food for you. Unless you've taken to eating catnip without telling me."

Grant pivoted toward my familiar, offering his hand to him to smell. "Good nose. The baker there has a cat herself, and recently added cat treats to her offerings." He glanced at me. "I hope it's okay that I got some for everyone."

Alphie sniffed his hand before allowing Grant to pet him. "Please say it's okay, Nora."

"I can't remember the last time you asked me permission for anything," I said, laughing. "Alphie, meet Grant. Grant, meet Alphie, my familiar."

After a brief hello pet, Alphie returned to me. Or rather the bag from the bakery. He sniffed it fervently.

"Let's see what he got, shall we?"

"Oh goodie!" Tilly chimed excitedly as she scooted behind Alphie trying to get closer to the bag but was blocked by all of Alphie's fluff.

"Another early talker, huh?" Grant asked.

"Yeah. Just those two so far." I peered inside the bag but was prevented from seeing much because most of the stuff was in small pastry boxes. "That's Tilly, Alphie's shadow." I reached into the bag and pulled out the one thing not in a box, a cellophane bag with a label marked *tuna treats*. Inside that were nine golf ball-sized puffed treats, almost like meringues. "Nine?"

"I knew you had the seven kittens, so I figured one for each and then two for Alphie since he's, well, not a kitten."

"Oh, I like him," Alphie said. "Knows how to get on my good side."

"You don't have a bad side when there's food involved." I rubbed his head.

"That was my plan, to win over your cats," Grant said, his voice low as he came up behind me. Warmth radiated off him like a just poured cup of coffee that I wanted to gently place my hands around to soak it in. Any more of this and I'd be like the whipped cream on top of one of my fancy coffee drinks, melting into a hot mocha, only it would be my heart melting for a cute crime scene tech instead.

Right. Coffee. "Would you like something to drink?" I spun around, thrusting the bag of treats into Grant's hands, before spinning away and fumbling for the coffee maker's on button. Okay, so maybe the jitters from his unexpected arrival hadn't left. Or maybe these were new ones entirely due to the closeness of his presence. Breathe, Nora.

"That would be great, thanks."

I pulled down another coffee mug, this one read *coffee is a magical brew*, and behind me, the treat bag crinkled. A moment later, Alphie and Tilly both said thank you.

"You, I know already," Grant said as I faced the kitchen once more. He placed a treat out in front of Sport and then one in front of Batley. Dodger joined his brothers on the floor and received his treat next.

"That's Whisk," I told him as he held out a treat toward the orange tabby. "She'll get on your shoulder like Dodger does if you let her."

A few feet away, more cautious than the others were Katie, the brown tabby, and Dolly, the calico. Grant held treats out to each of them.

"It's all right, you two. He's a friend." I smiled, liking the sound of that. "I don't have many people over when I foster on account of the possible talking." Gemma was the only regular even when I didn't have kittens around.

Grant gently rolled the two treats the remaining few inches to Katie and Dolly. Then he slowly stood and joined me at the counter, his side almost touching mine. "Thank you for letting me meet them."

"Thank you for bringing me pastry. I'm sorry about the notebook."

"It might be gone, but the information isn't."

"What do you mean?"

He lifted a hand and brought it to my temple, his touch featherlight as he tapped it with two fingers, the others gently moving a wisp of my hair in the process. "You said you had a photographic memory, right?"

I nodded, more aware of his touch than his words.

He gazed at me, his hazel eyes searching my face. "Then it's all in here." With one final tap, he lowered his hand, this time purposely moving the strand of my hair and tucking it behind my ear.

"I don't know how much I'll be able to remember. If I'm not actively trying to store it away, I can't recall it easily."

A stream of coffee poured into the pot, and Grant took a step back from me. I hoped I hadn't disappointed him. Again.

He reached for the bakery bag. "I believe in you. And your gift. Let's see what a little brain-boosting food can do."

"Then I probably should have had one of the cat treats. Fish is better for memory than baked goods."

He shook his head. "Kitchen witch, remember?" He pulled a small box from the bag, then opened it to reveal several mini-muffins. "These have been very popular with the school kids. They say they help them study and make recalling what they've studied easier."

I poured him a cup of coffee and slid it toward him so he could fix it how he wanted. "I'm willing to give anything a try." It was the least I could do.

"Glad to hear it. Then after that, we can celebrate with the pastries in the other box." His widening grin caused his cheek to dimple.

Feeling bolstered by his confidence, I poured myself a coffee and waved him over to the small table up against the far opposite wall of the kitchen. "Let me grab a notebook, and we can get started."

chapter
eighteen

Fueled by coffee and mini-muffins, Grant and I sat at the table while I flipped through the memory of the notebook page by page and copied down the information for him. As I worked, he photographed my copies, asked me questions as to the meanings of notes, and searched online for the symbols I didn't recognize. And the cats? Let's just say the catnip treats were a genius move on his part . . . minus the zoomies for the first twenty minutes of course. After that, they all settled down across the apartment, Alphie and Tilly by my feet and Dodger draped over Grant's shoulder.

Finally, after a couple of hours, we were done. I slid the notebook toward him.

"This is incredible," Grant flipped through the pages. "Is this even in your handwriting?"

I spun the notebook back toward me before shaking my head. "It's Dr. Loomis's."

"You'd be a magnificent forger. All this just from reading the notebook yourself? Imagine what you could do if you had spent more time with it."

My cheeks warmed at the strange compliment. "I don't

need time. It doesn't matter. Once I've seen it, I can pause on whatever it is, pull it out of the memory, look at it as close as I need to."

He blinked several times before speaking. "Recall is one thing, but manipulation of the things that you remember? That is so much more than a photographic memory." He released a breath, the word *amazing* floating across it.

If my cheeks weren't red from his comment a moment ago, they were now, but he was giving me too much credit. "It's still not as good as the real thing, though. I'm really sorry about losing the notebook."

Grant shook his head. "You didn't lose it. It was stolen from you. And what you just did will still go a long way in helping. It will verify the notebook as the right one once we do find it, and we will. I'm sorry your car was broken into."

I sighed. "At least fixing it won't be an issue."

He looked at me quizzically, and I explained how Dr. Loomis's husband offered to help.

His eyes widened. "And your car is there now?"

"Yeah. He said he'd be able to fix it no problem." His look didn't change. "Why are you looking at me like that?"

"He's back to being a suspect."

"In her death?" My chest tightened. Alphie, likely sensing this, bumped my leg with his head to remind me he was there. "But you said—"

"I know I discounted him before, but that was before finding out what his wife was poisoned with."

"Which was?"

"Antifreeze."

Ah. Now it made sense. "And you find antifreeze at car shops. Can't anyone buy that?"

"While that part is true," he started, petting Dodger's head, "few people need the particular kind that killed her, making that less likely. Have you ever had to add antifreeze to your car?" I shook my head. "Have you seen antifreeze before?"

A memory of standing in the driveway with my dad one late-fall Saturday surfaced to the forefront of my mind. I was young, almost five at the time, and he had the hood to our nineties station wagon open.

"Have to top things off," he had said.

"Then why are you draining that one?" I'd asked as he shimmied out from under the car. The sound of liquid pouring into the basin he'd placed on the ground next to him muffled his grunts as he moved.

"Gotta change out the antifreeze every thirty thousand miles."

In typical fashion of a kid that age, I'd asked him several more questions, giving the antifreeze enough time to not only be drained from its tank but from the engine block as well. When the process was done, my dad slid the basin out from under the car, added in the new bright-green antifreeze, and then poured the old stuff into the newly emptied bottle. "To keep animals and curious kids like you safe." He capped the bottle of used antifreeze. Unlike the new stuff, this old liquid was a greenish brown.

Grant gently placed his hand on top of mine, pulling me out of the memory. "What were you thinking about?"

"Just a random day doing car maintenance with my dad . . ." He didn't need to know the specific date, which I also could have told him. Though it wasn't really a random day. I'd learned something then, and now my face pinched in thought. "But I've driven way more than thirty thousand miles in my car and have never changed my antifreeze."

He smiled, and a low chuckle escaped him, causing my

stomach to flip-flop again. It certainly wasn't food poisoning. Not if the baker truly was a kitchen witch.

"I'm sure it's been taken care of during your inspections, but newer varieties for newer cars don't need to be changed as often. It's even a different color than when we were kids so people can tell the difference."

Following his train of thought, I guessed, "And the kind that poisoned her was the old kind?"

He nodded. "Way less likely for the average person to have these days."

"But not for a car garage."

"Exactly. So you can see why we need to look at her husband with a bit more scrutiny now. Think you're up for a small recon mission?"

"Me?" I bit on the inside of my lower lip.

"Not alone, of course. I'll take you to pick up your car, and if you can keep him talking, I'll try to poke around and see if I can spot some of the old-style antifreeze. It might not be enough for a warrant, but it would be corroborating evidence to support the possibility that he did this."

Alphie bumped his head against my leg once more, and I hung my hand down next to me, wiggling my fingers. A moment later, his furry head found them, and he walked enough so that the fur along his back tickled my fingertips before his tail became easy to grab. With a gentle stroke, I ran my hand to the tip of his tail, taming the floof and making it appear half its usual width. "You can do this," he whispered, swishing his tail this way and that as soon as it was out of my grasp, the fur fluffing out once more while a now-awake Tilly tried to grab it as if it were a toy. Then again, to her, it often was.

Dodger lifted his head off the front of Grant's shoulder

and sleepily added, "Yeah, you can do this," before flopping his head against the side of Grant's.

"For what it's worth," Grant said, "I agree with them. And who knows? You might see something I don't."

"Sure. Let's do it." If her husband did kill Dr. Loomis, then bringing him to justice was the right thing to do. And whether or not he did, maybe he'd be able to tell me something about why she had a notebook containing the names of familiars. Finding Dr. Loomis's killer wasn't my priority, but protecting the familiars was. If one led to the other, all the better.

A wide grin lit up Grant's face, switching the butterflies living in my stomach into the on position once more. "Thanks. Oh, I never get to do these with someone else. It will be fun." I raised my eyebrows—*fun?*—and Grant cleared his throat, dimming his excitement but not the fluttering sensation in my gut. "Did I say fun? I meant easy. This will be easy. I promise."

"Don't get to do this often, do you," I said, half teasing, trying to bring back some of the lightness he'd had moments before.

Pink tinged his cheeks as he shook his head. "I'm more the cleanup guy, coming in for the evidence."

"So you do the same sort of stuff for both the police and SISS?"

"Mostly."

"I'd love to hear about it sometime."

"Oh yeah?" This time it was his dimpled smile that made a return. Out of all the ones I'd seen so far, this was my favorite. "I'd be happy to tell you, and would now, but speaking of SISS, I need to head into the office."

I glanced at the digital display on the stove. "Now? Isn't it getting a bit late?"

Grant laughed. "It's SISS. They don't exactly have what

you'd call regular hours. Besides, how else would I be able to work for them and the Snowhaven PD if I didn't have a night shift for one of them?"

"You've got me there."

"When do you sleep?"

"I'm an efficient sleeper." I must have given him a look because a moment later he added, "And that's what all the coffee is for," with a wink. He lifted Dodger off his shoulder, much to Dodger's protest.

"Do you have to go?" he whined, echoing my thoughts.

Grant set him on the table and gave him a soft pat. "Unfortunately."

"Will I see you again?"

Grant glanced at me with a look I didn't recognize but liked. "Maybe."

"I hope so," Dodger said.

I hoped he would, too, and not just for his sake.

chapter
nineteen

Aside from being told my car wouldn't be ready for another day, thus delaying my recon mission with Grant for twenty-four hours, the first day splitting my shift between Feline Familiar and the animal hospital went by fairly uneventfully. Between the brisk walk between the two locations and the lack of coffee at the second, I collapsed into bed at a decent hour and fell right to sleep.

But the morning greeted me with chaos as I must have forgotten to fully latch the door to my bedroom closed the night before. Dodger and Batley zoomed over my chest, with who knows what toy in Dodger's mouth. I wiggled my fingers down by my side, finding Alphie's long fur where he lay curled in his usual spot by my hip.

"Why aren't you doing anything?" I asked him.

"This is your fault," he grumbled. "I'm pretending they're not here and maybe they'll leave me alone."

I slid my body up into a sitting position and found Alphie snuggled with Tilly. "Not pretending she's not here, are you?"

He mewed a laugh, sounding a little like when he'd get

water up his nose when he drank too quickly. "You think she'd let me?"

"He's just so comfy," Tilly chirped. "And it's not your fault. Someone has figured out how to open doors."

"Oh no, who?" Thank goodness I bolted the apartment door at night.

"It was more a group effort," she admitted after a moment. "Sport trapped himself in the bathroom yesterday going after a toy, and we all worked together to get him out."

"Speaking of being trapped, can someone help me?" an unfamiliar voice said.

I turned my head toward the sound as I tossed off the covers, spotting Whisk hanging in the window, one front paw on the curtain rod, the other with claws stuck into the curtain. While one back paw had gained hold of the screen, the other flailed to grasp the curtain as well.

I hustled off the bed and over to the window, then held her up with one hand supporting her chest as I worked on freeing her claws from the screen and curtain. "I got you, I got you."

"Thank you," she cried when the last claw came free a few minutes later, and I pulled her toward me.

"So, when did you start talking?" Three out of seven now. All early.

"Um . . . just now?" She pulled herself up onto my shoulder.

"Oof!" Alphie yowled, jumping to a stand and sending Tilly to her feet as well. Dodger and Batley scrambled out the door.

"My cue to leave," Whisk said before jumping off me and onto the floor.

The rest of the kitten crew followed close behind, Tilly included. I closed the door behind them, then turned back to a very flustered Alphie, his fur going all over the place. I gave him a quick rub down, laying his fur flat-ish for the moment. "Not sure how much longer I'm going to be able to keep this your kitten-free oasis."

"A lot of trouble. All of them," he grumbled, cranky because his morning nap had been cut short. No doubt if he was human, he'd be a coffee addict like me.

"I know you don't mean that . . . at least not about Tilly." I quickly got ready for my shift at Feline Familiar and packed a change of clothes for the animal hospital. It wouldn't be fully coffee-smell free, since I had to bring it inside with me instead of leaving it in the car, but it would be better than nothing. "Now come on, let's go get something to drink."

I had just enough time to down a cup of coffee before Gemma came to pick me up.

"Got a shipment coming in late morning," Amy announced to the crew before we opened for the morning. "Small batch. Shouldn't take long to unload, but I'll need help organizing the shelves once it's here to make room."

I glanced around the room, hoping someone else would volunteer. She regularly *voluntold* me for stocking duty because I was used to handling the bags of cat food and litter.

"What is it?" Gemma asked next to me.

I averted my eyes, pretending Amy wasn't looking my way. If it worked for Alphie in getting all but Tilly to leave him alone this morning—at least until Batley and Dodger ran over him—then maybe it would work for me.

Amy snapped her fingers. "You can be the first to find out. Thanks for volunteering."

"I should have known better," Gemma grumbled.

As it turned out, that delivery was for maple syrup. A whole lot of it.

"Something for the road?" I asked the delivery guy as he approached the counter once everything had been unloaded from his truck.

"Yes, please. Coffee. Black. Two sugars."

"Coming right up." I rang up the man, eyeing the logo on his baseball cap, a snowflake shaped like a maple leaf. Where had I seen it before?

The man paid me, then stepped to the side to wait for his coffee. Thank goodness for easy orders. I was already dragging but still had a half shift at the animal hospital to get through followed by a recon mission with Grant.

As Amy came up behind me so she could take care of our next customer while I grabbed the black coffee, I said, "Maple syrup, huh?"

An excited grin spread across her face. While not the typical summer flavor—usually early spring saw maple-based specialties throughout the Fiddlefern Fjord region, not summer—there was no doubt in my mind that Amy would come up with something great to make with it. Based on her smile, she already had. And given the size of the delivery, I envisioned several new food and drink offerings turning up on our menu in the coming days.

But her answer also explained where I had seen the logo the delivery driver sported without having to sort through those stored in my memories. Yesterday, when I put the rest of my iced coffee in the fridge at the animal hospital, there'd been a bottle of dressing on the top shelf with the Snow Maple logo on its label. Based on the name scrawled across the bottle in her handwriting, it had been Dr. Loomis's. She'd raved about it during the kittens' first vet visit. At least until I tried cracking a joke about tossed salad with her.

I poured the black coffee into our to-go cup and added the two sugars. After capping it, I swirled it around, incorporating the sugar, then set it before the delivery driver.

"You do that with all the coffees?" he asked me.

That would be a no. Usually I stirred hot drinks the regular way or let the customer do it. But that was the sort of day I was having apparently. "You should see it when there's edible glitter in the iced drinks. Wicked pretty."

"I'm not one for iced drinks, but I'll take your word for it."

"When did Snow Maple branch out and start doing dressings?"

His face scrunched as one eyebrow raised slightly. "We don't. Just the syrup and sugar." He thought for a moment. "And a couple spices. Maple pepper and stuff in that vein."

The memory played out before me. No longer than a flash because that's how long it was. One of many seemingly insignificant memories lodged in the depths of my brain featuring what seemed like a mundane task, grabbing something out of the fridge. But there it was, clear as day.

"Huh. I could have sworn I saw a bottle of maple vinaigrette dressing with that logo"—I pointed to his hat—"in the staff fridge at my other job." I certainly couldn't argue with the man who actually worked for the company that I had seen it, though. Maybe he was new. Or maybe it was a short-run batch sort of thing.

"Couldn't be from us, though it sounds good. I'll have to let my dad know about it. He's always looking for ways to expand the company."

Dad? Okay, so scratch the whole being new and not knowing all the products idea.

"Well, you can count on me as a future buyer of it for sure if you ever end up making it. Have a great rest of your day."

"You too." He nodded politely and turned toward the door.

Gemma came up and playfully hip-bumped me. "When did you turn into such a flirt?"

"Excuse me?"

"First the cute crime scene tech and now the delivery guy?"

"That? That was *not* flirting."

She raised an eyebrow at me and, in a voice an octave higher than her usual, said, "You can count on me as a buyer . . . If that's not flirting—"

"It's not!" I said, choking on a laugh.

"Mm-hmm . . . I wonder how Grant would feel to know he's not the only one you're flirting with."

"Gem-ma . . ." I groaned, walking around her and back to the register.

"Fine, fine. How is the cutie, anyway?" she asked as she wiped down the counter next to me. "You two have a rain date to make up for not going to Heartwood Hollow yet?"

"He's picking me up from the vets this evening." No need to fill her in on what else we were doing after.

She squealed in delight. "Speaking of the vets, shouldn't you be heading over there?" She shot a look over at the clock on the wall, and I followed her gaze.

"Oh, shoot, you're right. I still need to swing through the cat room to make sure all is good there, and then—"

"And then you'd have to hoof it to the animal hospital and still not make it on time. You go. I can take care of the cats."

"Are you sure?"

"You're not the only vet student here, remember?" she said, pointing at herself and bumping me away from my spot behind the register. "I just took an extra year to figure out that's what I wanted to do. Now go."

Already one step toward the back room, I slipped off my apron, telling Gemma thanks over my shoulder. She'd saved me a sprint to Familiar Friends, but I sure was missing my car all the same.

chapter
twenty

I flopped into the passenger seat of Grant's car.

"Long day?"

"You can say that again. This is only my second day splitting time between the café and the animal hospital, but I am beat. Thank goodness we'll be getting my car so I don't need to book it between the two again."

He passed me a coffee from Feline Familiar. "I had to guess what you might like. If you don't like it, I'd offer you mine, but it sounded good, so I got the same."

I sat up straighter in the seat as I took the coffee from him, staring openly at the man who was nervously looking at me, waiting for me to react to my first sip. The scent of cinnamon wafted toward me as I tipped the drink toward me, and the spiced-maple sweetness washed over my taste buds with the first sip. It was probably the placebo effect and not the espresso, but I was already feeling more alert. Or maybe that was from how Grant was still gazing at me as if his happiness at this moment hinged on my approval of his coffee choice.

"Mmm . . . so good," I finally said to put Grant out of his misery. His worry was quickly replaced by a dimpled grin. "I'd wondered what Amy was planning with the maple syrup when it was delivered earlier."

"A *meowchiato*."

"Ah, a cousin of her winter *macchigato* with horchata in it."

"I think I had that one." He lifted his cup. "Couldn't pass this up when I saw the name. So you like it?"

"Most definitely." I mirrored his sip with one of my own. "Exactly what I needed today."

"So does that mean you're ready for our recon mission?" he asked as he set his coffee back into the cup holder between us.

Mid-drink, I swallowed hard to answer him. "As I ever will be."

We made small talk as Grant drove us to the garage where Dr. Loomis's husband and potential murderer had my car. Destination aside, it was an enjoyable ride and nice to get to know Grant better. Although we'd spent a couple hours together the day before yesterday, we'd been focused on recreating the notebook, not chitchat.

But beneath the layer of conversation, I was keenly aware of why we were together right now, and as we drew closer to the garage, my pulse quickened, and my chest and throat felt tighter. Maybe the two shots of espresso that were likely in my coffee were a bit too much on top of my nerves.

After a few minutes, we pulled in front of Loomis Autoworks. Cars needing repair were clustered to one end of the small parking lot, tightly packed to maximize the minimal space. I didn't see my car. Hopefully that was a good sign.

The bell over the door chimed as Grant and I walked into the shop. A glassed-in area with a few chairs and a TV in the corner sat off to the side of the entrance. Ahead of us was a counter, and beyond that, a doorless opening led to a repair bay.

"Be right there!" Dr. Loomis's husband called from somewhere inside the repair bay, drawing my attention deeper inside it.

On a delivery truck lifted into the air was a very familiar logo. Snow Maple. Was this a second truck, or had the delivery driver I'd spoken to earlier ended his day early due to an issue? How many trucks could a small, family-run operation have? And was this just a coincidence, or could that maple dressing sitting in the refrigerator at the vet's be the key to everything?

I gently nudged Grant with my elbow and leaned my head toward him. "This might be nothing, but Dr. Loomis had a homemade maple-based salad dressing in a bottle with that logo on it," I said in a hushed voice.

"Maple would be a great way to hide the sweetness of the antifreeze," he replied, matching my tone.

"Do you think that's how he could have killed her?"

"Entirely possible. Think you can get me a sample of that dressing?"

"I can tomorrow."

A noise rumbled through the building, and the delivery truck slowly descended.

At that moment, Dr. Loomis's husband walked into the room, wiping his hands on a rag. "Sorry about that. Truck had a flat, and I was just about finished with it when you came in."

"No worries. I think that truck was making a delivery to the café I work at earlier today." I pointed toward it as Grant wandered away from me to do his part in the recon mission.

"Sure was," Dr. Loomis's husband began. "It's the only truck they've got. Small business and all that. Fabulous syrup.

My wife especially loved it. But, café?" He tilted his head slightly. "I thought you worked with Ingrid."

"Someday I might have. I'm still going to school to be a vet. The rescue I volunteer for brings the cats where she worked to get care, and she regularly came into the cat café where I'm a barista."

"Ah, now I understand. She liked that café. Always went when she needed some kitty time."

"Do you not have your own?"

He shook his head. "Allergic. Guess that's the only comfort is that we don't have a pet grieving her too."

I nodded understandingly, needing to pivot this conversation to keep him talking while Grant looked around. "She was a very talented vet, your wife."

"Thank you. She loved what she did. Only thing that would have made it better, she used to tell me, was if the animals could talk to her and tell her what was wrong."

Was that why she was interested in familiars? Because they could take part in their care? While their being able to talk took some of the guesswork out of things, it didn't change much of what we did or could do for them.

"I used to joke and tell her she should have been a princess in a cartoon movie. She would have loved that." He looked down at his greasy hands. "Though I'm no prince."

Was that grief talking or had he just given me a veiled confession?

I glanced at Grant, but if he wondered the same, he didn't show it.

"I'm sure you were to her," I finally said.

"Thanks," he smiled sadly. "Not sure if I believe that. Not sure if I was ever good enough for her."

Again I wondered if that was grief or guilt. The conversation I'd had with Tabby on my first day with the kittens resurfaced. She'd said that Dr. Loomis and her husband had been having problems. A possible motive? Had she made him feel like he wasn't good enough and he'd finally had it? Easy access to antifreeze—and no doubt the knowledge of what it could do to someone—gave him the means to poison her, and who he was gave him the opportunity. I hoped that if he kept talking, he'd eventually reveal that he had killed her.

But as he continued, there was nothing more said that suggested any marital issues in the slightest. Maybe Tabby was wrong. Eventually he asked, "Did you know she actually believed it might be possible for animals to talk?"

"What, with some sort of technology? Like those collars that allowed the dogs in that kids' movie to vocalize their thoughts?"

He shook his head. "She wasn't all that techy to come up with something like that. And to tell you the truth, she didn't like collars all that much, not for inside the home. Too much stuff to get caught on. No, the way she talked was she thought they'd be able to do it on their own once she figured out how to make them do it."

This had to be why she was staying late at the animal hospital. So her notebook was research? Figure out what patients within the practice could talk and then what, continue to observe them? Ask the animals outright? Not that they'd answer her. And then what? Force them to talk? Worse?

My spine tingled, and I fought a shudder at the thought of what worse meant. Wasn't going to go there.

"That's really interesting," I finally forced myself to say, hoping to get more information from him. Find the missing notebook, find her killer. "Was this something she was doing on her own?"

"No one at the practice wanted anything to do with it, according to her. They were nice and all, but she'd been looking for others who might think similarly. Even contemplated leaving for a research facility. Somewhere that wouldn't prevent her from looking into it." He sighed and leaned one arm against the counter. "Maybe it's something you could continue in her stead. You're still young. Maybe not so set in your ways like the others."

"I haven't decided on a specialization yet. There are a lot of things I'm interested in." No need to tell him that following in his wife's footsteps was not one of them, no matter her motives for wanting pets to talk. Magic like that couldn't be explained. But he hadn't fully answered my question. I shot Grant a look, and he made an almost imperceptible nod as if encouraging me to keep going. "Do you know if she'd found anyone to help her? In case I decide to look into it more and need someone to talk to."

He shook his head. "If there was anyone else, she never said. I just know they weren't at the practice if there was."

"Well, if I decide that's something I want to pursue, that will probably complicate things"—possibly in more ways than one—"but I'll definitely keep it in mind. Thank you."

Grant meandered back over to me, so I assumed he got what he needed. "All set?" he asked.

I glanced back at Dr. Loomis's husband. "Guess that all depends. My car is ready, right?"

chapter
twenty-one

After quickly grabbing the rest of my drink from Grant's car, Grant walked me around the side of the building to where my car sat parked, all windows once again intact.

"Thanks again for scoping things out with me."

"Small price to pay for the ride over here." I smirked. "And the coffee. Did you get what you needed?"

"Yeah. There's a supply of it on a shelf in the front bay. Visible at an angle over in the waiting area."

"That's good, right?"

"It's a start. What about you? You catch anything in that photographic memory of yours?" He reached up and touched my temple, playfully tapping it at first before running his fingers down a strand of my hair and then tucking it behind my ear.

As if only realizing what he had done, he looked away and dropped his hand back to his side as if my hair were on fire. Sure, we could pretend that never happened, though the image of his wistful gaze as his fingers glided along my hair was burned into my mind, and the whisper of the hair tickling the side of my face seared into my memory. And instead of filing it away as awkward things I hoped to never repeat, I found myself wanting to take Grant's hand and tell him to do it again.

Grant cleared his throat. "You seemed to be having quite the conversation with Mr. Loomis. I only caught parts of it. Anything that could help?"

I shrugged. "Maybe? Though talking about it here probably isn't the best idea. Do you want to get dinner or something?"

His eyes widened as his smile grew rich and robust with a tinge of sweetness, not unlike that of the meowchiato still in my hands. "Yeah, I'd like that. A lot actually."

Heat coursed up my cheeks at his admission. But there was one problem. "Do you have time? Do you need to head to SISS?"

"Not tonight. Wasn't sure how this would go and wanted to give it enough time. So I'm all yours."

I liked how that last part sounded way more than I wanted to admit. "Great! So where do you want to go?" I was terrible at choosing that sort of thing.

"What are your thoughts about Mexican?"

"Perfect. I knew I liked you."

Even in the shadow of the building, I could easily see the tips of Grant's ears turn red, and no doubt my cheeks matched.

Somewhere between the free chips and salsa arriving at our table, and the waiter returning to make fresh guacamole for us as an appetizer with more deliciously salty tortilla chips, my mind turned away from the excitement of being here with Grant and back to the recon mission.

If Dr. Loomis's husband had stolen the notebook, why had he offered to take care of my window? To eliminate any possible evidence, or to make sure the police never looked into it in the first place? To throw off suspicion? I shook my head. Something about all of that didn't make sense.

"You okay?" Grant asked, eyeing me as he dipped a chip into the salsa verde.

I grabbed a chip of my own and nodded cheerfully, trying to reassure him I was happy to be here, but after another moment when I wasn't sure that my gesture had satisfied him, I said, "I don't think he did it. He was inside the funeral home the whole time. He had no time to break into my car."

"Doesn't mean he didn't have someone do it for him."

"True, but I don't know . . . how would he have known it was me who took it? How would he know my car? I only just met him at the funeral."

He seemed to consider this. "Let's say he followed her to work that day, to make sure the antifreeze had done its job, and saw your car there. Presumably he's one of the few who knows about the notebook, so what if he put two and two together when he saw you go inside?"

"That still doesn't mean he had the opportunity to take it," I said, returning to my original statement. "He never left the funeral home."

"Are you sure about that?" He tapped the side of his head, which I took to mean it was time for me to play the memory out in my head.

Doing so wasn't necessary. I swallowed the bite in my mouth. "I didn't watch him the whole time, but he was in the receiving line and then in the front row during the service. His absence would have gone noticed by someone. Surely they would have paused the service without him."

"True. But that brings me to what I suggested before. Could he have had someone else do it?" Was this what crime solving was, talking in circles?

I shrugged. "Still, a lot would have to go right for him to know that the notebook was in my glove box versus at home or even in my purse. It's too big a risk to break into someone's car otherwise. Especially if convincing me to not call the police hadn't worked. Maybe he really was just trying to save me the hassle and a few dollars."

"He was right about the whole deductible thing. And police rarely collect much evidence from a car break-in. Dusting for fingerprints on a glove box is pretty much only something you see in movies. My memory isn't like yours, but I can tell you I've been called out only once to process a car for a smash-and-grab. And that was because of who it was and what got taken."

I found myself wanting to know all about his case, but that wasn't why we were here. Hopefully I'd have another opportunity to hear about some of the things he'd been involved in.

"What did you learn from your conversation at the garage?"

I recounted the conversation with Mr. Loomis, everything from him being aware of the maple syrup truck being the only one the company had to why his wife was likely keeping the notebook of familiars' names.

"So," Grant continued, using a chip in his hand to point, "if he didn't do it, then you have to ask yourself, who knows what your car looks like? Who knew you had the notebook? Who knew you were at the funeral? And who either wasn't interested in her research or didn't want her to do it at all? Perhaps enough to K-I-L-L her."

I sighed hard, knowing where he was going with this

because I'd been contemplating it too. Unfortunately, I had to. "As much as I hate to admit it, if Dr. Loomis's husband isn't her killer, the biggest suspect pool is at the animal hospital."

Getting that dressing had become even more important now.

chapter
twenty-two

Familiar Friends Animal Hospital had been back open for a few days now and was in full swing with its schedule. A regularly scheduled day off from the cat café meant that today was my first full day at the vet's. From the moment I'd walked inside the back room, I'd been sent this way and that. I'd spent the morning cleaning the dog run out back and then the cages used by overnight patients after they'd been picked up by their owners, followed by prepping cages for any patients who would need some sort of post-surgical monitoring today.

As a result, I hadn't had one moment to myself to sneak a sample of Dr. Loomis's salad dressing for Grant to test.

Although I was used to this sort of work from regularly caring for the cats at the café, I'd worked up quite an appetite for lunch. As soon as I finished my last cage, I dashed to the fridge to grab my food, knowing that this was also my best chance to get my sample of maple vinaigrette until I had to leave. Maybe my only chance.

This afternoon, if I finished all my work, I would get to observe a surgery. I wasn't certified to do them outside of the teaching hospital, but watching fell within all bounds of what I could do here. Definitely a perk of the job, right behind the free coffee at the other one. Though likely working with a killer put a damper on my overall enthusiasm for said perk.

With any luck, testing the salad dressing would get us one step closer to figuring out whodunnit. But when I opened the fridge, the bottle was gone.

"Hey, Tabs, where did that dressing go? The one you said had been Dr. Loomis's. I was hoping to try it. I love maple things."

Tabby lifted her head to look at me. "Oh that vinaigrette? She loved that. If it's not there, then either her husband took it or someone threw it out."

"Her husband?" The same husband who had easy access to the substance that killed her? And who mentioned his wife loving maple syrup when I talked to him yesterday?

"He stopped by last night to gather the few things of hers that were here."

The animal hospital was open later on some nights to offer more flexible scheduling for the patients. He must have come right after work. Right after I left after picking up my car.

"Poor guy," Tabby continued.

"Yeah . . ." Unless he was the one who poisoned her, but I wasn't going to tell her that. It would be all over the practice by the time it closed for the day. I ducked back into the fridge as dread blossomed in my stomach. The logo on that dressing bottle was the same as the one on the truck in the shop. Had our quick conversation about it reminded him to come by and get rid of evidence?

"Nora? You okay?"

"Oh, yeah. Just looking for something else I could use

instead." I grabbed a random bottle of dressing and made a show of pulling it out. "Is this okay?"

Tabby nodded, and I put it on the counter next to the fridge before grabbing my lunch. Committed to the act, I poured just enough dressing to be believable into the little cup I'd brought to collect a sample, wishing it was maple vinaigrette instead. Then I put the dressing back in the fridge and took my lunch to the tiny staff table.

"Enjoy," Tabby said, standing. "Back to the desk, I go."

I gave her a quick thanks and then dove into my lunch.

Between my disappointment over the salad dressing making me feel unmotivated and a Cairn terrier with an upset tummy, cleaning the exam rooms was taking longer than I had hoped it would. I still had three rooms to go, and at this rate I was going to miss the last of the day's surgeries. Even more disappointing, but at least there'd be other opportunities for that. But for testing the dressing and possibly catching Dr. Loomis's killer? Not so much.

As I restocked the paper towels, one of the screws on the dispenser seemed loose. Easy enough fix. I grabbed my multi-tool keychain from my pocket and adjusted it so the screwdriver was accessible. Only when I went to press the screwdriver into the screw to tighten it, it popped off completely, sending it skittering across the floor.

Since I couldn't leave it there for some cat to find and turn it into a toy, or worse, eat it, I got on my hands and knees to grab it under the bench where it had come to a rest.

Once I had it in my hand, I realized that although it had impressions on its top like a screw did, it wasn't one at all. Part of it was glass, and the screw-like portions were there to protect that glass—a tiny camera lens.

Thoughts of my conversation about security cameras with Tabby and Dr. Barker resurfaced. This wasn't supposed to be here. The coven hadn't installed cameras in the exam rooms. So who did?

Only one possibility came to me, but I couldn't ask her. She was dead. Was this how Dr. Loomis was collecting names for her notebook?

I pocketed the camera and finished cleaning the exam room before darting into the one I'd finished just prior. A mirror image of the one where I'd found the camera, its paper towel dispenser seemed like the obvious choice for a camera covering this room. I ran my finger up the side and found it capping one of the actual screws, one used to put the holder together, not messed with during the reloading of paper towels. It had probably been a coincidence that the one I'd found in the other room had gotten loose.

Whether this was the only camera in here, I had no way to tell. I'd have to ask Grant once I got back to my phone.

It took some time—I had to hop back into some rooms between appointments—but I collected cameras from every exam room at the animal hospital. I'd texted Grant during my patient updates to their owners, sending them all pictures of their furbabies staying with us for whatever reason, but I'd yet to hear back from him.

Armed with a pocketful of cameras, I knocked on the office door for the vets on duty, including Dr. Barker. The other was in surgery, one I was supposed to observe, but oh well, this was more important now.

"Dr. Barker?" I said hesitatingly when she didn't respond to my knock. She glanced up at me, and I crossed the tiny office to her desk. I placed the tiny camera in front of her. "I found this in the exam room. You said there weren't cameras in them."

"There aren't supposed to be any." Dr. Barker lifted the tiny thing and examined it. "So that's how she did it," she mumbled.

"Excuse me?"

"Oh, nothing." Dr. Barker shook her head quickly as if clearing a thought. "Thank you for bringing this to my attention. This is unacceptable. I'm going to call our security company. If it's not one of theirs, then hopefully they can tell me whose it is."

At that moment, Tabby came to the door with a card for Dr. Barker. "This got dropped off. From the owner of the dalmatian who got into a fight with the garden gnome."

Dr. Barker chuckled as she opened the card. "Such a silly pup. Thank you, Tabby." Then she opened up her desk drawer and slid the card inside before closing it again, but not before I saw the corner of a very familiar notebook.

Oh. My. Goodness. My mind raced back to the funeral home. Dr. Barker had been ahead of me in line, meaning she was done before me. And although she was sitting waiting for me once Gemma and I had finished, there would have been just enough time for her to sneak out the back door, break into my car, steal the notebook, and get back without me ever seeing her leave.

Although Dr. Barker knew about my photographic memory, and would thus know that I'd recognize that notebook anywhere, she gave no indication that she realized what I had seen. Instead, she said, "Is that all, Tabby?"

"Yep!" Tabby turned to leave, but stopped and looked at

me instead. "Oh, if you're really interested in that salad dressing, you could ask Dr. Barker about it."

I raised an eyebrow.

"She made it. Guess it's a specialty of hers. Right, Dr. Barker?"

"Oh. Thanks, Tabby," I tried to hide the sinking feeling from my voice as everything came together.

chapter
twenty-three

The picture I saw at the funeral of the dinner party at Dr. Barker's appeared in my mind.

Several things lifted up out of the photo as if now in 3D. It wasn't hard to fill in other parts of the scene since I'd been there before, though for a barbeque with other incoming veterinary students at the time and not a dinner party like this. Dr. Barker sat in one chair, flanked by students, and a pre-Dr. Loomis sat across from her, a heaping pile of salad on her plate. And next to the bowl were several bottles of dressing, including one with the Snow Maple logo on it. Had the event in question been the first time Dr. Loomis had Dr. Barker's maple vinaigrette? I'd never had it myself. Despite what I'd told Tabby about wanting to try it, I was much more a cream-based salad dressing person than a vinegar-based one. Not that I ate much salad to begin with. Nor was I about to start now after all this if my suspicions were correct.

And given the notebook in Dr. Barker's desk, they had to be.

With Tabby out of the room and heading back to the front desk, Morgan handling a patient in one of the exam rooms, and the other vet in surgery with our other tech, it was just me and Dr. Barker in this section of the building. Alone.

The words flew out of my mouth. "Couldn't you have just hexed her instead? The right hex would have sent her fleeing the practice if not Snowhaven or even Fiddlefern Fjord entirely."

"And let her continue her so-called research somewhere else? I don't think so," she stated devoid of any emotion, sending any doubt I had right out the door and a chill up my spine. "Or have SISS breathing down our backs for hexing a human? No way. Dealing with her had to be completely devoid of magic. Of course, you had to go and get them involved anyway."

Not that it had been intentional. Not originally. But speaking of SISS, I slid my hand into my scrubs pocket where my phone still rested from patient updates earlier. If I could activate the screen unnoticed . . .

I lifted my chin slightly, hoping to draw her attention to my face with the movement so I could do what I needed to in my pocket. "They would have gotten involved the moment it became clear she was looking into familiars."

"The coven would have handled it before they even had the chance to step in. You don't think we knew she was doing this? We were trying to find out who she was working with."

"By killing her?" No way would the coven have allowed that. The rule of three, that what we put out into the world comes back to us threefold, was a key tenet of our beliefs.

"No, by forcing whoever it was to make the next move and then catching them in a trap. You should have come to me with the notebook."

"So you could potentially hurt someone else?" I shook my head. "Dr. Loomis was dead. Here. And she had a notebook with the names of familiars in them. Had I not been here, the police would have found it. I took it to protect the familiars."

"I already had that covered."

"What do you mean?"

"I was down the street when you called." So that's how she'd gotten here so quickly. I knew that had seemed faster than just speeding would have done. "I'd planned to get here, find her dead, and take the notebook for myself. I was protecting the familiars too."

"There's a difference. I never would have killed Dr. Loomis. Or endangered others."

My phone vibrated in my pocket, and I pressed it tightly against my thigh to stifle the noise while also tapping where the answer button should be on the screen. Unable to see it, I hoped it was Grant on the other end, or at least someone who could get help.

Dr. Barker rolled her eyes. "I did what I had to." How could someone so concerned with saving lives be so blasé about taking one?

"So you poisoned her salad dressing? What if someone else used it?"

She shrugged. "Collateral damage. Not like anyone would have used it while she was alive. She wasn't one to share. You saw her name all over it. Goddess forbid anyone else touch it once I gave it to her. Besides, you saw that it was gone today. I couldn't let *you* eat it."

"Thank you, I guess. I wasn't going to eat it, though. I wanted a sample to test for antifreeze."

"Well, aren't you a surprise . . . Now let me ask you something. How did you figure out it was me? I'd hoped to frame her husband for it."

She thought I'd pegged her as the killer before walking in

here? "I didn't know. Not until Tabby said you made the salad dressing and I saw the notebook that you stole out of my car in your drawer." Had I not found the camera and gone digging for more, I wouldn't have had a reason to come in just now. Though Tabby might have told me about her making the dressing eventually.

"You always have been very observant." A smug grin crossed Dr. Barker's face. "It would have served you well as a vet."

"Served? Just because my professor turned into a murderer doesn't mean I'm not going to become a vet."

"Well, unfortunately," she tsked, "I can't just let you walk out of here now that you know what I did."

I stepped back toward the door as she reached into her desk once more and pulled out a syringe. My heart pounded in my chest as I contemplated the myriad of substances she could have put in there that could kill me. Words from my textbooks and names on bottles from the veterinary pharmacy in the back of the animal hospital floated in my head. None were pleasant. "You don't have to make this any worse than it already is."

"Oh, it will be sad. Two deaths of veterinarians with bright futures ahead of them in such a short time. But we'll soldier on."

She flicked her hand, and the blind on the office door flew closed. I'd heard of her telekinesis powers but had never seen them before now. I took another step back. If I could get around the other side of the filing cabinet a few feet away, then I could push it over to create an obstacle for her to get around. Hopefully that would give me enough time make a run for it.

Then she lunged for me and missed, landing hard on the floor and throwing all my planning out the window. Before she could try again, I pulled the filing cabinet down, hitting her and pinning her leg to the floor.

I dashed to the door as she screamed, and I threw it open.

Gemma and Tabby stood in front of me. Gemma pulled me into a hug and to safety as she stepped out of the doorway. "What are you doing here?"

"You texted me, and I was on break so I called you back. I heard the whole thing. I heard her confess." If it wasn't Grant that I'd reached, Gemma was the next best option.

At that moment, Morgan rushed out of her exam room and the other vet came flying out of surgery with her tech. "What is going on here?" the vet cried.

"Collateral damage, huh?" Tabby yelled as the syringe went skittering across the floor. "I should have used that on you, but I'm no murderer."

Gemma hugged me tighter. "I called Tabby using Vicki's phone. She heard everything too."

"Thank you." I squeezed her back then stepped out from her embrace to face the other two. "Dr. Barker killed Dr. Loomis. Antifreeze in her salad dressing."

The vet gasped, and tears sprang into Morgan's eyes. Based on their reactions, they were shocked to hear the news. And if that were true, I doubted what Dr. Barker had said about the coven being aware of Dr. Loomis's actions. Maybe she had hoped they would shield her once they found out, but no way would they have condoned murder.

Tabby strode out of the vet's office, wiping her hands together. "She won't be going anywhere now." We all turned to stare. She chuckled. "At least until the police show up. Or SISS. I'm not sure. It depends on who your boyfriend brings with him." She'd directed that last part at me.

"Grant?"

She nodded.

"He's not my boyfriend." Why that fact mattered at the moment, I wasn't sure.

"Well, whatever he is, he brings his cat here. I looked up his patient record and called him while I had Gemma on the other line. Should be here any minute."

chapter
twenty-four

Grant had been working in the PD lab when Tabby called. He tipped off SISS while alerting the rest of the Snowhaven force, and within minutes of everyone at the animal hospital learning the truth, officers arrived to arrest Dr. Barker for Dr. Loomis's death. Additional charges had been brought up by SISS. And of course the coven was involved too.

Two days after the incident, I'd met with the high priestess and other coven leadership to give my side of events. They claimed no knowledge of Dr. Barker's plans or even what Dr. Loomis had been looking into regarding the familiars. A potential research partner was something to keep an ear out for, but with no leads or actual confirmation that she wasn't working alone, there was nothing we could do at least for right now. But I'd been assured that Dr. Barker would not be welcomed back into the coven for what she'd done to Dr. Loomis and what she'd tried to do to me.

A week had passed since the arrest, and the gossip was finally dying down among the workers at the café, but the staff at the animal hospital was still processing. No doubt it would take them some time.

I'd still been splitting my shifts between the two jobs and was as busy as ever. But today was a rare day off from both places as all seven kittens were being fixed. The talkers at Familiar Friends and the ones who had yet to talk—if they ever would was still unknown—at the veterinary school's learning clinic.

Once they had recovered, it would be time for them to head to the cat café's catio to meet the residents and wait for their forever homes, where they would live out their days as witch's familiars or as cats for non-witches.

Except for one.

Tilly was staying with me and Alphie.

He really had grown attached. And although he was by no means old for a cat, he was adamant that training my next familiar was going to take some time because thinking about making my coffee hard enough for the maker to come on and brew me a cup was hard to master.

And speaking of coffee . . .

"Order for Grant and Nora?" the tattooed, dark-haired barista called from behind the counter of Leafs and Grounds, the coffee shop in Heartwood Hollow.

We approached the woman, who slid us our drinks.

She pointed at a small counter a few feet away on the opposite wall. "Anything you could want to add to your drinks is right over there along with caps and stirrers."

"Thank you," I said, picking up my cup and nodding appreciatively.

Grant and I headed to the small condiment station, where we each capped our cups without adding anything. Call me a coffee purist, but unless it was plain black coffee, I wanted to enjoy my fancy drink exactly how it was made for me. I hadn't asked him, but we'd discovered over the last week that we shared a lot of the same tastes, so I wouldn't be surprised if he thought the same.

Together we left the coffee shop and turned toward Main Street and the small bakery on the opposite side of the road. We were finally getting to check out that bakery run by a supposed kitchen witch. After the delicious mini-muffins the day I recreated Dr. Loomis's notebook, we knew we'd have to come back for more. That and the cats had been clamoring for more of those cat treats Grant had picked up for them that day. We figured surprising them all with some after their surgeries would help them feel better.

"So I've been meaning to ask you something," Grant began.

I glanced at him as we crossed the street, and my pulse quickened at the slight upward curl of his lips. "Oh?" My voice practically cracked on the simple word.

We stepped onto the sidewalk, and rather than head right on into the bakery, the door already open and the smells from inside wafting out to greet us, Grant stopped.

"I was wondering if you would like the idea of me adopting Dodger." He sounded so nervous and wouldn't look at me, but I sure did want him to. I doubted my smile could get any bigger. Dodger would love that.

"You see," Grant continued, still looking at his feet as he toed the cement, "I've gotten rather attached to him during the couple of times I've seen him. And maybe Batley too? I know they pal around together. And I think they'd be a good fit with my guy at home."

If we both didn't have hot coffees in our hands, I'd have thrown my arms around him. Instead, I did the next best thing. I stepped toward him, lifted onto my toes slightly, and gently kissed his cheek. "I love the idea."

He met my gaze as I stepped back, and his hand slowly rose to his cheek, now tinged with pink, as he smiled sheepishly. "I'm really glad you do."

"And what's more important is Dodger and Batley are going to love it. I can't wait to tell them." I grabbed his hand and pulled him toward the front step of the bakery. "Now come on, there's something warm and chocolaty calling my name."

He stopped me again as I reached the step. "One more thing."

I spun to face him. "Wha—"

His lips crashed into mine. Not hard, more rushed, as if he didn't just go for it, he would have chickened out. But the surprise was worth it. They were warm, and soft, and tasted slightly of the single sip of toasted vanilla almond cookie latte he'd gotten at the coffee shop. Or maybe that was me. We'd gotten the same thing. Again.

All too soon, the kiss was over. Grant pulled away, eyes hooded, and his once sheepish smile now lit up his face. I'm sure it matched the one on my face.

And did the bakery lights just get brighter?

Grant seemed to notice it too. "Interesting."

"Shall we go in?" They probably thought we were weird for standing out here so long.

He motioned for me to go in, and we stepped into a brightly colored bakeshop full of pink, purple, and yellow accents.

"Hi, welcome to Suncraft Bakery," a woman around my age wearing a purple apron said. She stood behind the counter, a warm, knowing smile on her face. What it was she knew, I wasn't sure. "I'm Joanie, and I have got to say, you two are such a cute couple."

A second woman came through a door in the back, holding a tray full of brownies. "And she knows a thing or two about that."

Joanie chuckled. "That and we might have seen you two through the window." Heat flared in my cheeks, and a quick look at Grant revealed pink rising all the way to the gentle tips of his ears. "Ah, still new, I see. Well, what can I get you?"

My embarrassment was quickly replaced by my excitement over baked goods. I pointed at the brownies the second woman was loading into the case. "I'll have the biggest brownie you've got. For here, please."

"Sarah, hand me a brownie, will you?" Joanie said, holding a small plate out to Sarah. She then looked at Grant expectantly.

"One of your mini orange pound cakes, please."

As she rang us out, I asked, "Do you have any of your cat treats, by chance? He was here last week and brought some to my foster kittens, and they loved them."

She pointed to a rack in the corner of the room. "Foster kittens, you say?"

"Uh-huh. They're all getting fixed today, so I figured I'd surprise them all with more treats once I get them home."

"Aww, well you go grab a bag. My treat."

Tray emptied, Sarah stood up. "Good thing Ivy isn't here. She wouldn't leave you alone until she heard all about your kittens."

"Who's Ivy?" I asked, genuinely curious and a little hopeful.

Joanie's eyes crinkled at the corners as she answered, "My boyfriend's daughter. She's almost eight and has been on him about getting a kitten for a while now. He's liable to break any day."

Could I really get four of the kittens homes before they even left my care? That would be great. And if Joanie was a kitchen witch, she had to know something about familiars. "I have seven. Well, three are spoken for now, so four left. They'll be at Feline Familiar, the cat café in Snowhaven, starting next week once they've all recovered."

"I'll let him know. Her birthday's coming up, and I wouldn't be surprised if he finally caves."

Grant and I took our goodies to a table across the room and sat down. I moaned—literally—in delight at the first bite. Still warm, the perfect mix between chewy and firm, with soft but not too melty chocolate chips.

"You have got to try this," I told him.

"Same." He slid his plate across the table to share a piece of his.

Oh my goodness. It was just as delicious. A sweet, tangy orange in a not-too-dense cake with a sweet orange sugar-glaze frosting poured on top. I wasn't sure I wanted to give it back.

He must have sensed my reluctance. "Split them?"

I nodded eagerly, and we swapped halves, then both took combined bites of the two baked goods.

Life the last several weeks since becoming the kittens' foster familiar had been busy, and no one could have expected the events of the last couple of weeks. In another week or so, the kittens would be out of my apartment, and things would calm down even more. But as I looked across the table to find Grant gazing back, I knew that for other things, this was just the beginning.

Rosie Pease

Nora and her foster familiars will return.
In the meantime, continue your stay in Fiddlefern Fjord, home to Snowhaven, Heartwood Hollow, and more with one of Rosie's other cozy books.

what's next?

Looking for a new mystery staring another cat from Feline Familiar? Trouble lives up to his name in *Catastrophe on the Road*, prequel to the Purrfect Travel Companion series. Nora's friends Gemma and Amy both make an appearance as does a certain crime scene tech.

Curious about Joanie, that kitchen witch in Heartwood Hollow? She's a matchmaking baker living in a town that's full of secrets. Start to uncover them in *Cookies and Curses*, Book 1 of Mixing Up Magic.

***Catastrophe on the Road* and *Cookies and Curses* are both available now.**

about the author

Rosie Pease is a native Rhode Islander who has also lived in Vermont, New York, and Ohio. She uses the places she's traveled to as inspiration for the settings of her cozy mysteries, pulling the theater from one, the cider mill from another, and the river from yet another to create fictitious towns that feel familiar.

She collects Funko Pops of the Doctor Who, DC TV, and Marvel variety, with a few others thrown in for fun. Her desk is a mess, but she can find everything on it, so it works for her as long as things aren't falling onto the keyboard as she writes.

When she's not crafting cozy mysteries, she's playing with her daughter, hanging out with her husband, or being amused by her two catnip-loving ginger tabby cats.

Come find Rosie online:
Website: https://rosiepease.com
Facebook, Instagram, Threads, X, and Pinterest:
@WriteRosiePease

also by rosie pease

The Matchmaking Baker
Coffee and Calicos
Sweets and Santa

Mixing Up Magic
Cookies and Curses
Scones and Spells
Weddings and Witchcraft
Potluck and Powers
Muffins and Mediums

Perfect Travel Companion
Catastrophe on the Road
Catastrophe in the Kitchen

Feline Familiar Cat Café
Foster Familiar

Tales from Haunted Heartwood Hollow
"The Tree Monster of Dunmore Falls"
"The Holiday Hellcat"

Be sure to sign up for Rosie's newsletter to stay up to date on future releases.

www.ingramcontent.com/pod-product-compliance
Lightning Source LLC
LaVergne TN
LVHW040102080526
838202LV00045B/3737